"There's some
about before we t
any further," Dan

Tory paused. Th
suggest that everything she'd felt with Dan and
believed he'd felt with her was trivial. "What
should I think about?" she asked quietly.

"That I'm not a sweet guy," he answered, suddenly agitated. "I can be a bastard, Tory. I'm the
kind of man somebody should have warned you
about."

Tory smiled. "I know that. You're the kind of
man every female is warned about the minute
she becomes aware that boys aren't exactly like
girls. I considered that before I decided I'd rather
have one glorious night with you than spend the
rest of my days regretting I didn't. But Dan, you
most certainly are sweet. You're an absolute
dear, whether you choose to think so or not."

"A dear," he repeated. "I'm sweet, a regular
Knight of the Round Table. Tory, when it comes
to men, you're twenty-five going on fifteen."

She smiled. "Could be I'm too inexperienced for
you. So maybe my falling asleep in the car was a
blessing in disguise—"

The rest of what she'd planned to say was lost
in the hot recesses of Dan's mouth. Cupping
one hand behind her head, he laced his fingers
through her hair, then kissed her with wild
abandon, more intimately than any man ever
had. . . .

WHAT ARE *LOVESWEPT* ROMANCES?

They are stories of true romance and touching emotion. We believe those two very important ingredients are constants in our highly sensual and very believable stories in the *LOVESWEPT* line. Our goal is to give you, the reader, stories of consistently high quality that may sometimes make you laugh, sometimes make you cry, but are always fresh and creative and contain many delightful surprises within their pages.

Most romance fans read an enormous number of books. Those they truly love, they keep. Others may be traded with friends and soon forgotten. We hope that each *LOVESWEPT* romance will be a treasure—a "keeper." We will always try to publish

LOVE STORIES YOU'LL NEVER FORGET
BY AUTHORS YOU'LL ALWAYS REMEMBER

The Editors

Loveswept® 574

Gail Douglas
The Lady Is a Scamp

BANTAM BOOKS
NEW YORK · TORONTO · LONDON · SYDNEY · AUCKLAND

THE LADY IS A SCAMP

A Bantam Book / October 1992

If you would be interested in receiving protective vinyl
covers for your Loveswept books, please write to this address
for information:

Loveswept
Bantam Books
P.O. Box 985
Hicksville, NY 11802

ISBN 0-553-44205-8

Published simultaneously in the United States and Canada

Bantam Books are published by Bantam Books, a division of
Bantam Doubleday Dell Publishing Group, Inc. Its trademark,
consisting of the words "Bantam Books" and the portrayal of
a rooster, is Registered in U.S. Patent and Trademark Office
and in other countries. Marca Registrada. Bantam Books, 666
Fifth Avenue, New York, New York 10103.

PRINTED IN THE UNITED STATES OF AMERICA

OPM   0 9 8 7 6 5 4 3 2 1

To "The Brat"—who's anything but.

One

Dan Stewart leapt to his feet and went to the window behind his desk to adjust the blinds. The sun was streaming in on the woman opposite him, threading her hair with gold and studding her eyes with amber sparkles, and Dan wanted it to stop—needed it to stop. Maybe then he could think like a businessman again.

"Miss Chase, your presentation has been extremely . . . interesting," he said as he tried to shut out the light. "And I must admit your credentials are impressive."

"Why, thank you," she said in the husky lilt that somehow made a melody of every syllable she uttered.

Dan darted a glance over his shoulder at her, noting the flicker of amusement in her eyes and the sassy little smile tugging at the corners of her mouth. A mouth that kept making him think of dusky pink roses about to blossom. A lovely, tempting, distracting mouth.

When she saw that she'd been caught like a schoolgirl making a face behind the teacher's back, she didn't do the normal thing and feign a bland expression. She let her smile burst into full bloom.

She began to speak, and Dan was entranced by the way her lips formed the words. "Mr. Stewart, I can't help feeling that you have some reservations about my proposal," she said.

Dan nodded appreciatively, then realized what he was doing and gave his head a little shake. "What? What makes you think I have reservations?" He had several, but he hadn't voiced them.

"The word *interesting*," she answered, then laughed softly. "It's what you tell a struggling actor friend backstage after a real turkey."

Dan stared at her, nonplussed. She was a little too perceptive. Turning away again, he noticed that he was still fiddling with the blinds. He dropped his hands to his sides. There was no point trying to block out the light when the real radiance was coming from inside.

He stood peering through the hairline openings between the slats like a neighborhood snoop, while he tried to figure out how to explain the unexplainable.

It wasn't difficult to rationalize his doubts about hiring Victoria Chase's event-planning agency to add sizzle to one of the most crucial product launches in the ten-year history of his company. She was too young for that kind of responsibility—no more than twenty-five, unless he missed his guess. Her track record was impressive but short, her agency the smallest and newest in Santa Barbara. And he wasn't sure he ought to entrust a pivotal assignment to someone with such an impish grin.

But rationalizations had nothing to do with the truth, which was simply that the moment Victoria Chase had come bouncing into his office, his heart had done a backflip. The soft waves of her collar-length hair had made his fingers tingle. Her feminine curves, intriguingly emphasized by her tailored green suit, had made him want to hang a Do Not Disturb sign on his office door. He felt as if he'd been searching for her through several incarnations and suddenly he'd looked up to see her materializing right before his eyes. He'd heard choirs singing and bells tolling. His world had turned into a Frank Capra movie, and he didn't like Frank Capra movies. Sentimental claptrap.

"Um . . . Mr. Stewart, is there anything you want to ask about my presentation?"

Dan gave a start but remained at the window without turning. "No, I have no questions, Miss Chase. But there are a few considerations to be . . . considered." Great start, he thought disgustedly. Eloquent. But he was committed now, he had to keep going. "The thing is, when a firm with a certain profile in business equipment makes a dramatic directional shift to interface with a revised target market . . ." His voice trailed off as he realized he'd been reduced to spouting the worst kind of computer gibberish. Had someone drugged his morning coffee?

He cleared his throat and tried again. "We do need a dramatic image change for the sake of the leisure and household items we're adding to our product line, but we have to be cautious. We're still very strong in business systems, so even though we want to show our lighter side now that we're moving into household robots, electronic toys, advanced computer games, and so on with our electronics division, we have to reassure our established customers of our continuing seriousness and our solid foundation. We have to . . . to walk softly . . ."

"And carry a big shtick?" she said helpfully.

Turning once again to stare at her, Dan almost choked on his sudden intake of breath. He didn't crack a smile even though he liked her mild irreverence. He was too bowled over. Victoria Chase was amusing, but the way she made him feel was no laughing matter.

While he was gaping at her she picked up her purse and briefcase and got to her feet. "Mr. Stewart, thank you for considering Happenings for such a crucial function," she said with the sweet smile that kept jamming the gears of his mind. "But we both reached a decision several minutes ago, so let's not prolong this discussion."

Dan blinked. Had something gone wrong with his hearing? *She* was turning *him* down?

Returning to his desk at last, he rested his fingertips on the polished surface and leaned forward. "Miss Chase, I don't believe I've uttered a word about a decision," he said with what he knew was chilling softness. The book he'd read about management by intimidation hadn't been a total waste after all. He waited for her to sink into her chair and keep quiet until he was ready to dismiss her.

But Victoria Chase didn't seem to understand her role. Her smile widened and a curious warmth appeared in her eyes. "Let me put it this way," she said in a kindly tone. "I'm sure you'll agree that it's as important for me to know I can work with you as for you to be satisfied I can do the job. I think you'll also agree that we don't . . . well . . . *mesh*."

"Mesh?" Dan repeated, dumbfounded. "You're saying you don't *want* my account? Because we don't . . . *mesh*?"

She offered her hand. "I knew you'd understand, Mr. Stewart. Thank you again for thinking of Happenings. I wish you every success."

Too thunderstruck to speak, Dan accepted the

handshake and immediately wished he hadn't. Victoria Chase's firm grip was no surprise, but he hadn't been grounded against the jolt of electricity her touch sent surging through him. His one consolation was that she seemed equally shaken, her flush deepening from pink to all-out crimson as her gaze locked with his.

They stood staring at each other in shocked silence until, emerging from their trances at the same instant, they broke apart as if just realizing they'd had hold of something so hot, it burned.

Victoria Chase turned, marched smartly across the pearl gray carpet, and left without a backward glance.

"I blew it," Tory announced twenty minutes later as she strode into the office she shared with Elizabeth Collins, her partner at Happenings and her best friend since they'd met in college.

As she hung her purse and suit jacket on a coatrack, Tory sighed heavily. "I lost the Stewart account, Liz. Or I turned it down. Take your pick." With the faint hope that she could get away with only that much explanation, she rattled on, "How are you doing with the Hart wedding? Do they really want to get married in a hot-air balloon?"

Liz looked up from the raft of papers that covered almost every inch of her desk's turquoise surface. Pushing back her straight blond hair, she peered at Tory through her enormous glasses. "They want balloons for all their guests as well, and for a string quartet. Now, *what* did you say first when you breezed in here?"

Resigned to offering more details, Tory plunked her briefcase down on her own desk and faced her partner. "I turned down the biggest account we've ever gone after." She began pacing back and forth across the width of the cramped room, too jumpy to sit down. "I had to. Stewart was trying his best to be nice about it, but he was going to show me to the door. I decided to let the poor man off the hook before he embarrassed us both by stumbling his way through an entire dictionary of corporate jargon that basically added up to 'No way, José.'"

There was a long silence before Liz gave a low, throaty laugh. "So you made it easy for him to turn you down."

"I couldn't help myself, Liz. He obviously didn't feel comfortable about giving me the contract, and it bothered him to tell me I wasn't going to get it. I felt sorry for him. He was just so . . . so . . . sweet."

"Sweet?" Liz repeated, raising both eyebrows. "Are we talking about Daniel J. Stewart? The man who's made the giants of an entire industry sit up and start sweating in their Brooks Brothers suits? He didn't bite off a nice little chunk of the electronics market by being *sweet*. He's a barracuda! And there's something I should tell you right now—"

"He's not a barracuda," Tory interrupted, stopping in her tracks. Then, wondering why she was leaping to Dan Stewart's defense, she laughed self-consciously and resumed her restless pacing. "Okay, I admit he's not the friendliest person I've ever met. And from the minute I walked into his office I got strange vibes from him. I had the impression the only reason he was giving me a hearing was that Roger McCormick had asked him to—one of the first things Roger did, I gather, after signing on as Stewart's marketing VP."

Stopping again, Tory looked down at the emerald linen suit she'd worn for the interview, the black patent-leather shoes, the understated gold accessories. So much for dressing for success, she thought, sighing. "Who knows what went wrong? Maybe the man hates green. Or brown hair. Or short women."

"Or short brown hair," Liz said with an odd little smile.

Tory grinned and tugged on one wavy strand as if to hurry the slow growing-out process that had begun the very day she'd made the mistake of letting her hairdresser talk her into a cropped look. "Could be. I'm not too fond of it myself. Anyway, it was a case of rejection at first sight. I felt like a fool going through the motions while Stewart sat there like a Greek statue with a great tan." She laughed again and finally retreated behind her desk, flouncing so forcefully into her fuchsia swivel chair, it spun a half turn and nearly dislodged her. "I wouldn't be able to work with Stewart anyway," she said as she grasped the edge of the desk to steady herself. "His account may be a plum, but he's a prune. His perfect face would splinter if he forgot himself enough to smile, and he works at being intimidating—"

"Whoa," Liz cut in, sliding her glasses down her nose to peer over them. "What happened to *sweet*?"

"He is. I said he *works* at being intimidating. I didn't say he was successful at it. But he's such a sobersides, Liz. No humor at all."

Liz studied Tory for several moments. "And he's dangerously attractive," she ventured.

Tory shifted uncomfortably in her chair, then swiveled to face the window behind her, staring absently at the poster of the Santa Barbara waterfront she'd taped to the glass to hide the stucco wall that was her actual view. "I suppose he's good-looking, if you go for the brooding, blue-eyed Gypsy type complete with black hair and sardonic brows." And the minute she'd walked into Daniel

J. Stewart's office, she added silently, the laser beam of his steel blue gaze had triggered a meltdown instead of the deep freeze she was sure he'd intended. She twirled to face Liz again. "Anyway, I made my pitch and I blew it, whatever the reason."

"Not exactly," Liz murmured, taking off her glasses and polishing them with a tissue she'd plucked from the box beside her.

Tory's antennae shot up. "What aren't you telling me?"

"I *tried* to tell you, but you were too fired up to listen. Roger called just before you came steaming in here like the little engine that couldn't. You landed the account."

Blanching, Tory gaped at her partner. "Are you serious?"

"I'm afraid so. Of course, if you really don't care to add Stewart Enterprises to our client list, call Roger back and tell him his boss is the stumbling block. There's no need for you to deal with a stuffed shirt whose magnetism makes you uneasy."

"Magnetism? I didn't say anything about magnetism," Tory said, adding a disdainful sniff for good measure. "And of course I'll take the account. What makes you think I wouldn't?" She shot her partner a teasing grin. "Honestly, Liz, where do you *get* these wild ideas?"

"What happened?" Tory asked Roger McCormick when she arrived for her first meeting with him in his spacious corner office at Stewart Enterprises. "How did I end up with this account?"

With a wave of his hand to indicate the sitting area at one end of the room, Roger answered, "I assume you gave your usual dynamite presentation."

"Oh sure, dynamite," Tory repeated with a roll of her eyes.

"You also happen to be a small enough agency to be able to move fast, without a lot of committee meetings and red tape. We're on a tight time frame here," Roger pointed out.

"I noticed," Tory commented. On her way to the luxurious arrangement of leather chairs and marble-topped tables, she looked out the huge picture window onto a *real* panorama of the Santa Barbara waterfront. "Hey, being a marketing VP has its perks, Rog. Your view's almost as great as mine," she said with a grin.

Roger laughed. He'd been in Tory's office, and he'd seen her fake view.

As she sat down on a low-slung armchair, Tory smiled at Roger's struggle to arrange his gangly body in the chair opposite her. After planting his large feet on the floor and leaning forward with his elbows on his knees and his hands clasped loosely together, he glanced toward the doorway, did a double take, then stood up again.

Tory's gaze followed his, coming to rest on Daniel J. Stewart in the flesh—the gorgeous flesh. She swallowed hard. Before she could censor her thoughts she found herself wondering what he looked like under his impeccable tailoring. Lean, obviously. Hard. Taut hips and thighs—no question about that. She mentally replaced his suit with form-fitting jeans, took off his shirt and tie. Nice. Her mouth suddenly felt dry and it was a struggle to breathe. She was shocked. What in heaven's name was happening to her? She didn't do this sort of thing!

Daniel J. Stewart was a menace. He had no right to look so attractive and be so stuffy.

"Sorry," Dan said.

You should be, Tory said silently.

She realized that his glance was moving over her at a leisurely pace, as if he were checking out a new purchase—or trying to remember whether he'd ever seen her before. It was futile to try to guess what was going on in his mind. She only hoped he had no idea what had been going on in hers.

"I didn't mean to break in on a meeting," he said after a silence that had lasted much too long, then nodded to Tory. "Nice to see you again, Miss Chase."

"Tory," she corrected him, rebelling against his internal formality even though she was pleased that he remembered her.

"Tory?"

"Short for Victoria."

"I see." His gaze locked on hers with such intensity, she found herself wondering breathlessly just what it was he *did* see. It annoyed her that she wanted him to see something he liked, such as the way she looked in the yellow Anne Klein dress she'd blown a small fortune on at a discount designer shop the previous afternoon. Did he approve? Did she care? She pleaded the fifth.

"What can I do for you, Dan?" Roger said, his bemused tone cutting through the crackling tension.

Dan gave Roger a surprised look, as if he'd forgotten his vice president's presence. Then he made a vague, dismissive gesture with one hand. "It's nothing urgent. I'll catch you later. Your meeting with Miss Ch—" He stopped and cleared his throat. "Your meeting is more important."

Then, as suddenly and quietly as he'd arrived, he was gone.

"Who *was* that masked man?" Tory whispered, convinced that Dan Stewart did wear a mask, one he probably never took off. She couldn't help wondering what he was hiding. Or hiding from.

"Strange," Roger said, sinking back into his chair. "Dan doesn't barge into my office unannounced if he thinks someone's with me. And he knew you were scheduled for this time slot."

"I guess he forgot," Tory said in a small voice, still staring fixedly at the spot where Dan had been, as if half expecting to see a ring of blue smoke curling up from the floor.

"Dan doesn't forget," Roger insisted. "From what I know of him, he doesn't forget anything, ever."

Tory pulled herself together and grinned. "There's always a first time, Rog. Now let's get down to some serious planning. We have to come up with an event that'll rattle the cage of this revised target market we're supposed to interface with, and we have to do it fast."

Roger gave her a strange look.

Tory laughed and opened her briefcase. She knew that Roger was aware of her usual impatience with corporate jargon, but she didn't bother explaining where she'd picked up the buzzwords and why she'd chosen this particular time to use them.

Two

Tory kicked off her shoes and dragged her swivel chair over to the bookcase that dominated the long side wall between Liz's desk and hers. One of these days, she vowed, she was going to remember to buy the stepladder she'd been promising herself since she and Liz had set up their office. They'd furnished it with an eye to using every available inch of space, including cabinet tops and high shelves, and Liz wasn't always around with her five-seven stature to get things down from high places.

After wedging the chair against the wall, Tory hitched up her straight skirt and boosted herself up. Balancing precariously with the toes of one foot digging into the chair seat and the other perched on the back to give herself a bit of extra reach, she curled the fingers of her left hand around the edge of one shelf to hold herself steady, then stretched to get at a wicker basket just beyond her fingertips. When she realized the effort was futile, she grabbed a book from a lower shelf and started batting cautiously at the basket, trying to nudge it closer without sending it and its contents flying.

A sound behind her made Tory glance over her shoulder, hoping Liz was back from her meeting. A rescue at this point would be welcome. But it wasn't Liz she saw in the open doorway. "You!" she cried, startled into taking too hard a swipe at the basket. It toppled over, spilling its cache of hand puppets on her head. As she lost the center of gravity on her chair, it did what it was designed to do: it swiveled.

Tory made a quick decision to let go of the shelf and try to hurl herself free of the chair, rather than risk dragging everything down with her. She hadn't much hope of landing on her feet, but it was worth a try. "Watch out!" she cried as Dan Stewart dropped the thick manila envelope he was carrying and plunged forward.

He ignored her warning and looked as if he planned to catch her, but the timing was off and, thanks to the determined push she'd given herself, Tory cannoned into him so hard, she was sure he was going to hit the floor with her. Under her, to be precise. The prospect didn't horrify her as much as she thought it should.

But she'd underestimated the man's strength. Slamming into him was like colliding with an armored truck. Although he did swear softly and reel a little, he managed to keep his balance and fold his arms around her to keep her steady, even when a spotted purple-and-neon-pink frog rolled out of the basket, flopped down onto his head, and slid to a grinning stop on his shoulder.

Tory's first thought was that Dan Stewart smelled good. Spice with a hint of lime.

Her second thought was that he might be a stuffed shirt, but the stuffing in question was solid, perfect for nestling against.

Her third thought was that she'd better banish the first two and find out what Daniel J. Stewart was doing in her office.

Before she could find out anything, however, she had to salvage whatever dignity she could from this fiasco. After taking a deep breath so she wouldn't sound too much like Minnie Mouse, Tory forced herself to tip back her head and smile up at her newest and most forbidding client, at the same time flattening her palms against his chest. "Why hello, Mr. Stewart," she said brightly. "What brings you here?"

Dan stared down at her, seriously worried. He'd found a feeble excuse to see this woman for the express purpose of testing his reactions. Well, he'd tested them. And he was as electrified as he'd been the other two times. He was also perplexed. Obviously Tory operated on the theory that the best way to handle an awkward situation was to pretend nothing unusual was happening. All right, he decided, he could play along. "Roger mentioned that he was going to send you our hot-off-the-press product brochures, and since I happened to be coming over this way I offered to drop them off," he explained calmly, feeling proud of himself.

"Oh," Tory said in a small voice, her bravado fading fast as her body began letting her know how much it liked the position it was in. The strong arms wrapped around her weren't letting go. The azure gaze locked on hers was like the promise of a bright sky behind dense storm clouds. The mint-scented breath fanning her skin was as warm as a midsummer breeze, and the lips hovering just over hers were an invitation to undreamed-of delights. Oh yes. Her body was enjoying itself immensely.

Suddenly Tory realized that her lips were parting. She moistened them with the tip of her tongue. *Good lord,* she thought, *he's going to kiss me.*

What brought her to her senses was the stunning knowledge that she just might kiss him first. "Are you all right, Mr. Stewart?" she said hastily. "I didn't knock the wind out of you, did I?"

He gave her a startled look, then released her and stepped back as if just noticing he'd waded into the surf without taking off his shoes. "I'm fine," he answered, his tone abrupt. He removed the frog puppet from his shoulder and gingerly placed it on her desk. "How about you?"

Tory awkwardly smoothed down her coral linen skirt and tucked in the silk blouse that had slipped free of her waistband. "No harm done, thanks to your timely arrival." She thought she was being quite gracious, considering she could easily blame her unexpected visitor for causing the mishap in the first place. "I was lucky you happened along when you did," she added without a grain of sincerity.

"Yes you were, Miss Chase."

Tory's eyes narrowed as she watched him adjust his navy blazer and straighten his striped silk tie. "I beg your pardon?" she said quietly.

"You are lucky I happened along when I did," Dan answered. "You could've broken your neck."

Tiny copper flames appeared in Tory's eyes. "But I didn't, so all's well, as they say," Tory muttered, grabbing the fuchsia chair and rumbling it back to its place behind her work table. "It so happens I've climbed up onto swivel chairs before, Mr. Stewart. Also folding chairs and any number of other odd perches, and this is the first time I've fallen."

"Then you're fortunate, Miss Chase." Gradually working up a full head of steam, Dan began pacing back and forth in front of the table, still shaken from the scare she'd given him and the heat that had shot through him like a fiery arrow the instant he'd felt her sweet little body landing on him. "I couldn't believe my eyes when I started into this office and saw a grown woman pulling such a harebrained stunt!" His long strides took him from one side of the narrow office to the other and back several times, stopping only when he almost smacked his nose into a small pink rabbit with blue plastic eyes and a buck-toothed grin.

"Did I hear you mention a harebrained stunt?" it asked in a sassy voice that imitated Dan's own intonations and speech mannerisms. "Hare-brained, Mr. Stewart? Is there an implied criticism of rabbit intellect in your comment?"

"No, it was an explicit criticism of a certain young woman's common sense," Dan shot back, then raked the fingers of one hand through his hair. "Oh terrific. Now I'm arguing with a piece of pink fake fur."

"The name is Cecil, Mr. Stewart, and I am no more a piece of pink fake fur than you are a conglomeration of snakes and snails and puppy dog tails." Tory knew she was carrying her teasing a little far, but she figured she had nothing to lose except an account she didn't want. Dan Stewart was disturbing her sleep already. Much more exposure to him could be hazardous to her mental health. Besides, she was curious to see whether sheer outrageousness would coax even a hint of a smile from him. "You could be more sensitive," she made Cecil say as she shaped his mouth into a pout. "Rabbits have feelings, too, you know."

Dan tilted his head to one side and studied Cecil, then cocked one brow at Tory. "You're good," he said thoughtfully. His gaze went to her mouth. "Do your lips move?"

"Do yours?" she countered with a sudden tremor. He wasn't supposed to look at her that way. It wasn't fair.

Dan allowed himself five seconds to imagine his lips moving over hers, then took issue with her question. "Why do you ask? I'm not the one playing ventriloquist here."

Tory removed Cecil from her hand and leaned him against a vase of flowers on her desk before dropping to a crouch to gather up the puppets still strewn all over the floor. "Does your mouth ever turn up at the corners, Mr. Stewart?" she asked as she filled her arms with colorful creatures. "What does it take to make you smile?"

"I smile," Dan said, frowning as he retrieved the manila envelope he'd dropped earlier. "I smile a lot."

Troy chose not to say anything more on the subject.

Dan wasn't ready to let it go. "If I was supposed to be amused by seeing you fly through the air with the greatest of ease, Miss Chase, let it be said here and now that I'm not into amateur acrobatics or slapstick humor."

She stood up, clutching an armful of colorful creatures. "Okay. No flying somersaults or pratfalls. Now, would you do me a favor? Would you use your superior height to get down that basket I was after in the first place? The world is cruel to short people. We have to take chances and put up with difficulties you six-footers never dream of." She thrust out her chin and added, "Including being talked down to by certain people."

Dan bit back a retort as he put the envelope on Tory's desk. He noticed the ocean view from her window and was puzzled for a moment. The office building wasn't anywhere near the waterfront. He looked more closely, then raised his eyes heavenward, shook his head, and went to get the basket that had spilled its contents on them earlier.

"Thank you," Tory said primly when she'd dumped the puppets into the basket and placed it on her desk.

"I like your office," Dan said, for some reason trying to make up for his earlier condescension. "All these bright colors . . . the offbeat touches . . . I feel as if I've wandered into the middle of a Saturday-morning cartoon. It's refreshing."

"Hardly your style, though," Tory commented, still feeling slightly defensive.

"We all have to present ourselves and our surroundings in a certain way, Miss Chase. You happen to be in a business that allows you a bit more freedom than mine does. Now, if you were an accountant . . ." He picked up one of the puppets. "May I ask you something? I'll try not to be patronizing."

"I didn't say you were patronizing."

"Yes you did. And I suppose you were right. But to get back to my question, Miss Chase, what's with the hand puppets?"

"I don't have any friends," she couldn't resist saying. "I get lonely, so I've had to create my own social set."

"Okay, now that you've got the kidding around out of your system, what's the real answer?" Dan asked patiently. "Or am I too curious?"

"Actually, I wasn't kidding. Well . . . I was, but I was telling the truth too. When I was growing up my family moved around a lot, so I did find it hard to have friends."

"And you did get lonely," he murmured, fighting the insane urge to take Tory Chase in his arms and cuddle her.

"A little," she admitted, wondering why she was chatting so freely to a man she wanted as little as possible to do with. Yet she continued, "I used to commune with invisible kindred spirits. I guess my folks heard me and thought it would look better if I were talking to something—anything. So they gave me my first Cecil, the great-grandaddy of this one. My menagerie grew over the years, and I learned a smattering of ventriloquism and mimicry. It all helped when I started out in the function-planning business by organizing children's parties. I still handle a few kids' bashes, but only the old-fashioned kind, not the flashy exercises in excessiveness."

"You refuse to handle glitzy affairs for the junior set? I hear they're pretty lucrative."

"They are, and I have nothing against going all out for youngsters. I just don't want to contribute to creating jaded six-year-olds."

"So you're off to do your own brand of *The Muppet Show* this afternoon," Dan remarked, increasingly unsettled by the things he was discovering about Tory Chase. It was one thing to be powerfully attracted to her, but he didn't want to start liking her too much as well. The combination could lead to some kind of emotional connection. Complications and connections. He didn't like them. Especially where women were concerned. "I didn't realize my function planner still got involved in actual performances," he added absently.

His function planner, Tory thought, wishing she could resent his proprietary phrasing instead of feeling a treacherous thrill skittering up her spine. "I retired my act a year ago, except for family and charity occasions."

"Charity occasions?" Dan said, his interest caught.

"You know—visits to hospital pediatric wards, that sort of thing," Tory said with a dismissive shrug. She didn't like to talk about her efforts to cheer up the lives of youngsters who needed it. She felt she did far too little of that sort of thing, the heavy demands of her business cutting deeply into her free time. "Anyway, the magician I'd hired for a little boy's birthday this afternoon has the flu, so I'm going to fill in with my puppets."

Dan looked at the selection of whimsical creatures and marveled at the wild imagination that had gone into designing them. "Where did you get these things?" he asked.

"I made them," Tory answered, then grinned as she looked at them from Dan Stewart's staid perspective. "I guess you find them pretty weird, huh?"

"Pretty weird, yes. But wonderful," he said. "Kids must love them. Do you play all these parts? So many different characters represent a lot of voices."

Tory laughed. "Heavens, no. I do Cecil and play around with a few extra voices, but mostly I let the children take turns working the puppets and talking for them. It helps them break the ice with one another and gives them a chance to stretch their own imaginations."

Dan picked up several creatures and closely examined them. He toyed with the thought of letting Tory in on one of his most closely guarded secrets, if only to shake up her apparent image of him as a humorless drone. But he resisted the temptation and zeroed in on the frog that had landed on his shoulder. Thrusting his hand inside the body, he tried working the pink-lined mouth, at first just opening and shutting it, then scrunching it up in various ways and finally positioning it in a horrible sort of smile. "Is this frog the kind that turns into a handsome prince if you kiss him?" he asked casually.

Tory's pulse lurched. Was Dan Stewart flirting with her? Impossible. But just in case . . . "Frogs never turn into handsome princes," she said with a sparkle of mischief in her eyes. "That rumor was started by some ambitious amphibian with a yen for royal smooches, a flair for self-promotion, and no scruples about false advertising."

Dan raised one dark brow and studied Tory for a long moment. "Do I detect a note of cynicism?" he asked at last.

"I don't think so. Realism, maybe."

"Realism." Dan glanced at the frog puppet on his hand and nodded. "Yes, I can see how important realism is in your life."

Tory couldn't help laughing. "So I have a few lapses. What can I say?"

"That you'll have lunch with me."

Her heart screeched to a stop. Had Dan Stewart just asked her out to lunch, or was she hearing things? Come to think of it, had Dan Stewart just made her laugh? The Bad Humor Man himself? Of course, she hadn't made *him* laugh. That was a whole other challenge.

"Tory?" he prompted.

Good lord. Now he was using her first name. Things were moving too fast. "Lunch?" she said in a small voice. "When?"

"Now, naturally. It's noon and I assume you have to eat, so I thought we could go somewhere and talk over a few ideas for the product launch."

"I don't have all my ideas worked out yet," she protested. "How could I? You just gave me the brochures with the descriptions of the new lines."

"I wasn't referring to your ideas," Dan said firmly. "I have a few of my own I'd like to discuss with you. Of course, if today isn't convenient, we can get together another time."

"Today's fine," Tory said. After all, he *was* the client, she told herself, so if he wanted to take her out for a harmless little lunch to force-feed her his hackneyed ideas, she might as well get it over with. With a fleeting smile, she finger fluffed her hair, grabbed her purse, and started for the door.

"Miss Chase," Dan said.

Tory turned. Back to last names, she thought with a stab of regret. "Yes?"

"Aren't you forgetting something?" Dan asked, cocking one brow.

Tory looked around. "Do I need my briefcase? I have a notepad in my purse."

Dan shook his head and hunkered down on one knee. "You might want to slip these on, Cinderella," he said as he picked up one of her shoes and held it so she could slide her foot into it.

Mortified, Tory swore under her breath. But she decided to take the line of least resistance and let Dan play Prince Charming. Probably it was a novel experience for him.

The fact that he was extremely adept at sliding a delicate high-heel shoe onto a woman's waiting foot was something she preferred not to think about—even when his hand, lightly touching each of her ankles in turn, sent coils of heat twirling all the way up her legs and through her whole body.

All of a sudden a simple meeting over lunch seemed about as harmless as sending Granny to the movies and inviting the Big Bad Wolf in for tea.

Three

"Leapin' Lizards?" Tory said when she stepped inside the offbeat restaurant Dan had chosen, a converted warehouse with a giant hot pink iguana peering over the edge of its roof as if watching for a human it could scoop up for a light snack. "You chose a place called *Leapin' Lizards?*"

"Don't let the name put you off," Dan said, enjoying Tory's surprise. She'd been too quick to jump to conclusions about him, claiming he never smiled, implying he had no sense of humor, telling him she didn't want to work on his account because they didn't "mesh," whatever the hell she'd meant by that. He had no idea why he wanted to shake up her misconceptions, but he intended to do it—without revealing the one detail that would prove he had a lighter side. "The food's great," he went on blithely. "The salsa has a kick to it, the guacamole's smooth, and the blue corn chips are the best in town. And the Newt Burger? Oh man, there's nothing quite like a Newt Burger."

Tory stared at him, her expression dubious. "A Newt Burger? Isn't a newt a . . . a reptile?"

"I was kidding," Dan said, rolling his eyes.

"You? Kidding?"

"Another one for *Ripley's*," he shot back.

Tory ignored the comment. "And you've been to this restaurant before?"

"Many times. Haven't you?"

She shook her head as she took in the colorful surroundings. The psychedelic creatures perched on the pale yellow walls and lurking in the cactus plants looked like bigger versions of her puppets, so it seemed logical to assume that the place had been chosen for her sake. Yet it wasn't Dan's first visit. "I've never seen this restaurant before," she murmured. "I've never even heard of it."

"It opened a couple of months ago," Dan explained, then nodded to the perky blond hostess who greeted him by name and showed them to what she called his usual corner.

Tory kept looking around, her eyes huge as she took in the scarred wooden tables and brightly painted chairs, the Navajo rugs and the clusters of plants, and above all, the menagerie of papier-mâché desert creatures conjured up from some-one's off-the-wall imagination.

When they were seated she couldn't help voicing her amazement. "Don't get me wrong, Mr. Stewart. I think this restaurant is delightful. But you? In these surroundings?"

"Why not?"

Tory lifted her shoulders in a little shrug. "It's so casual. It's designed for people who know how to have a good time."

"You think I don't?"

After pondering the question for a moment, Tory smiled. "Maybe you do, but I'd have expected your idea of a good time to be lunching in some chic, exclusive spot. Or better still, in a businessmen's club where everybody sits around in leather chairs interfacing about the target-market notches on their alligator briefcases."

Dan found it fascinating the way Tory's melodic voice and twinkling eyes could take the sting out of her most impudent comments. But he wasn't about to let her get away with poking fun at him, even if his pretentious speech during their initial meeting deserved lampooning. He was the client, after all. He had to establish limits. He pinioned her with a level gaze. "Touché, Miss Chase," he said quietly. "I have been known to slip into the verbal quagmire of computerese, but only in moments of extreme agitation. I'll try not to do it again."

Tory swallowed hard and felt the heat of a blush sweeping over every inch of her skin. Disarmed by Dan's bluntness, she let down her guard. "Touché yourself, Mr. Stewart. But I was the one on the hot seat during that interview. Why should you have been agitated?"

"Good question," Dan said, then made no effort to answer it. His attention had been drawn by the heightened color of Tory's creamy skin. Watching the flush inch down her throat to the shallow vee at the collar of her shirt, he found himself picturing how far the rosy hue would travel and what intriguing hills and valleys it would cover.

As Tory saw the direction of Dan's gaze and guessed the direction of his thoughts, her heart started skipping beats like the off-tempo cadence of a drunken bongo player. Beginning to have trouble breathing, she'd have undone the top button of her shirt if there had been one. On the other hand, as the steel blue eyes remained focused on her, she had to resist the urge to pull the edges of her collar together and ask the waiter to find her a safety pin. Several safety pins.

Annoyed at herself for allowing her troubling client to throw her into a tizzy, Tory cleared her throat and tried a new line of conversation. "What does the *J* stand for?"

Dan dragged his gaze and his thoughts away from their enjoyable meandering. "I beg your pardon?"

"The *J* in Daniel J. Stewart. What does it stand for?"

"What do you think it stands for?"

"I have no idea. Is it *Jonathan*? You don't look like a Jonathan, but you act like one."

"How does a Jonathan act?"

"Like you. Serious. Sober. No nonsense. By the way, why do you keep throwing my questions back at me? I can understand that a man who's made his mark in a cutthroat industry like yours tends to play close to the vest, but being secretive about your middle name is going a bit far, isn't it?"

"Let me respond to your questions and comments in order," Dan said with deliberate gravity. "The *J* doesn't stand for *Jonathan*. I toss questions back at you because I'm curious about your answers. I do have a habit of playing close to the vest, which could be the reason I've survived in this cutthroat industry. But I wasn't being secretive about my name. I simply wondered what you might guess. Now do I get to ask you a pertinent question? Or perhaps an impertinent question, like the ones you tend to come up with."

"Of course," Tory said warily.

"Thank you. Here it is. Why are you so determined to get my hackles up?"

Tory caught her breath. "Am I?"

"Determined? Yes. Succeeding? Not yet."

The warning was clear. Tory decided to heed it. "Could we start over?" With another swift glance around the restaurant she ventured, "This really is a super place."

"I like it," Dan said.

Neither or them spoke again for several moments.

"Well, so much for that topic," Tory said when she couldn't stand the silence any longer.

Dan looked around for a waiter, caught one's eye, and motioned him over, then folded his arms on the table and said, "Hang on, Miss Chase. The cavalry's on the way. I imagine we can fill a good three minutes discussing the lunch specials."

She laughed and relaxed a bit. The waiter arrived just as it dawned on her that Dan Stewart had amused her a second time. He might not be ready for Second City, but perhaps he did have a dry sense of humor hidden under those immobile features.

By the time she'd given her order Tory had made a decision. There was something she had to know, something she didn't feel she'd found out from Roger McCormick. As soon as the waiter left she smiled tentatively at Dan. "At the risk of succeeding in getting your hackles up, I do have another question I'd like to ask. I'm not sure whether or not you'll consider it impertinent."

Dan braced himself. What now? "Live dangerously, Miss Chase," he answered. "Fire away."

"What made you offer me your account after I'd suggested we wouldn't work well together?"

Treacherous ground, Dan mused. He had no intention of admitting that Tory's abrupt exit had shocked him into realizing he'd been allowing personal feelings to cloud his business judgment. She didn't need to know that he'd have preferred to keep their relationship on an unprofessional basis, that he'd have hired someone else except that Happenings was the right agency to plan this particular event. "Maybe I just don't cope well with rejection," he said after a moment's consideration. It was an honest answer in its way. He *didn't* cope well with rejection.

Tory smiled. "Nobody does, Mr. Stewart. That's why I turned you down before you could turn me down."

"I know."

"You know?"

"I'd have done the same thing in your position." Dan didn't bother mentioning that the real reason she'd turned him down was that she'd taken pity on him and handed him an easy out. "Why were you so certain of what I was planning to do?" he asked instead.

"Because my whole presentation was based on taking a lighthearted, humorous approach to your product display, and I couldn't jolly a smile out of you to save my life. I couldn't even get your full attention."

Dan found it hard to believe any woman could be so unaware of her effect on a man, but he was sure Tory wasn't being coy. He doubted that she was capable of it. "Obviously you'd won more of my attention than you realized," he remarked.

Tory nodded. "It seems I had. I guess I underestimated you, Mr. Stewart."

"I'd like to think so, Miss Chase."

The waiter arrived with corn chips, a mug of Mexican beer for Dan, and a glass of iced tea for Tory.

"You still haven't answered my question," Tory said after they'd clicked glasses and toasted the success of the project ahead. "Why did you give me the nod? I know you weren't going to."

"How can you be sure? You went huffing away

from that interview without waiting to find out how it might have turned out."

"I did not huff away."

"You huffed, Miss Chase. I know a huff when I see one, and yours was a first-rate huff. But to get back to your question, you won the account for the simple reason that you're the best person for the job. Perhaps you want more details. I know Roger has outlined why your agency was selected, so I have to assume you're just being female, fishing for compliments."

"For shame, Mr. Stewart," Tory said, then pursed her lips for an exaggerated tsk-tsk. "I wouldn't have expected such a sexist comment from you."

Watching the rounding of her full, soft lips and the dancing lights in her eyes, Dan was tempted to demonstrate to Tory Chase just how sexist he could be if he put his mind to it. But since he didn't plan to get involved in that way with a woman who threatened the self-control he'd nurtured all his life, he carried on with their light banter. "Anyway, Miss Chase, suffice it to say that I decided you must be very good at what you do. Given your penchant for telling a potential client to stick his account in his ear, you couldn't have survived for the two years since your firm's start-up if you weren't an outstanding event coordinator."

"I think that's a compliment," Tory said with a slight frown. "But for some reason I'm not sure."

"You're an independent woman," Dan observed. He picked up a corn chip, dipped it into the salsa, and impulsively reached across to hold it up to Tory's lips. "To a fault, some people might say."

She crunched into the salsa-laden chip and chewed thoughtfully. "Some people would be wrong," she said after she'd swallowed. "Independence is never a fault."

"Mmm. That statement is open to debate. How do you like the salsa?"

"Great."

Suddenly they both froze, staring at each other as they belatedly realized that they'd just shared an intimate moment.

"Jeremiah?" Tory said in a small voice after several charged seconds.

Dan answered without hesitation. "No, not *Jeremiah*. Why is my middle name so important to you?"

Because trying to guess it gets me out of some of the most awkward situations, Tory almost confessed. Instead, she managed a strained laugh. "If I don't get the right answer, there's this huge pile of straw I have to spin into gold overnight."

"Don't worry. I can assure you I'm not Rumpel Q. Stiltskin's brother Jumpel," Dan said, his expression deadpan.

Tory burst out laughing, as much from nerves as amusement. But it struck her that Dan had caught her off guard with his wry humor a *third* time. She was just getting used to that surprise, when she noticed that he was gazing at her with a penetrating warmth and a strange, faraway expression that wasn't funny at all. "Mr. Stewart?" she murmured.

"I was just thinking," Dan said softly. "Spinning straw into gold should be a cinch for Tory Chase. Everything around her seems to take on a special luster to begin with."

Tory's breath caught in her throat. "Oh, Mr. Stewart," she said in a ragged whisper.

Suddenly he scowled, a muscle in his jaw tightening. "At least, that's the kind of thing I've heard from people who've worked with you, Miss Chase, so I'm counting on you to weave your inimitable magic for Stewart Enterprises. We're risking our corporate neck with this move into the new lines, and that's no exaggeration."

"I understand," Tory said, deciding that her imagination must have slipped its moorings and floated off to Never-Never-Land. How could she have thought, even for a moment, that Dan Stewart's remark was more personal than a reference to her event-planning skills? "I know we have to strike the proper balance between whimsy and serious intent, Mr. Stewart," she went on. "You mentioned that you have some thoughts on the approach we should take?"

Grateful that his lapse into sappy romanticism had gone unnoticed thanks to his quick recovery, Dan settled down to brass tacks. "The main thing I wanted to do was suggest the names of some staff people you might want to talk to. Roger is new, so I don't expect him to know which of our resident mad geniuses would be most helpful—or where to find them at any given moment."

Tory dug into her purse for a pen and notebook and began writing as Dan talked. She took notes all through lunch, jotting down names and stray thoughts of her own as well as Dan's. The time whizzed by, and it was Dan who suddenly glanced at his watch. "When are you due at that children's party to take over for the sick magician?"

Tory looked at her own watch. "In less than half an hour. I'm sorry, but I really must go."

"Of course. I didn't mean to keep you so long," Dan said, signaling for the check. "How was your burger, by the way?"

"Terrific. And a big relief," Tory admitted. "Even though you said you were kidding, I was half afraid it really would be made of ground lizard.

You know how restaurants are these days. Chefs will serve anything just to be different."

"True," Dan agreed. "But if there's one thing you can count on with me, it's that I'll never take you to a place with that kind of chef. My taste buds are too traditional."

Tory gave him a bemused smile, then looked down and began gathering up her belongings.

Dan frowned. He knew she was puzzled about his comment. There was no reason for him to take her anywhere. Perhaps she even realized he'd manufactured the excuse for this lunch. He could have given Roger the information to pass on to her.

As he took his billfold from his breast pocket and extracted a credit card, Dan promised himself he wouldn't kid himself again about this woman. He would stay in the background where he belonged and let Roger take care of all communication with Happenings. He would put Tory Chase out of his mind and drive her from the dreams she'd crept into with her expressive eyes, her spell-casting voice, her infectious smile.

"All set?" Dan said, pushing back his chair and getting to his feet.

Tory shot him a surprised glance. "Yes, but . . ."

"Was there something else you wanted, Miss Chase?" Dan asked, perfectly willing to linger all afternoon but aware that she had to hurry away.

She shook her head. "Nothing *I* wanted, Mr. Stewart," she answered, then looked pointedly at the credit card lying on top of the bill the waiter had left but hadn't collected. "Aren't you forgetting something?"

Dan sat back down. "I guess my mind was elsewhere. I was trying to figure out the best way for you to get in touch with Howard Beecher." A weak recovery, he thought, but a recovery.

"Howard Beecher," Tory repeated, skimming through her mental files of the people Dan had mentioned. "He's your top researcher, right?"

"Right. The problem is that Howard doesn't show up at the office on a regular basis. He works at home as often as not, and his home is in Ventura." He pulled a business card from his pocket and wrote on the back. "Here's his address and phone number," he said, handing the card to Tory.

Dan's matter-of-fact statement about Howard Beecher's whereabouts was yet another surprise for Tory. Dan Stewart might be a pin-striper, but she was learning quickly that his ideas weren't strictly by the book. It seemed that the tight ship he ran was an unusual one. "Are you saying, Mr. Stewart, that you let some of your people work from home?" she asked after the waiter had picked up the credit card and hurried away to process it.

"Yes, if they want to, and if the logistics allow that kind of flexibility."

"You don't feel it's necessary to keep them under supervision?"

"Anyone who needs a lot of supervision doesn't work for long at Stewart Enterprises," Dan answered. "Besides, Howard Beecher has been with me since I started this company, and he's the main reason for its success. He could lie around his house watching soaps all day every day and still be an asset. He earned his salary for life a long time ago. The fact that he keeps coming up with brilliant ideas for us is a bonus."

"Good heavens, a corporate leader who gives as much loyalty as he expects," Tory said softly, more to herself than to Dan. "It's like finding out there really is a Santa Claus."

"Why am I getting the impression you have a low opinion of corporate leaders in general?"

Tory gave a little start, shocked by her outspoken comment. "I'm pleasantly surprised by your attitude, that's all," she mumbled awkwardly, then tried a quick diversion. "Is it okay with you if I get my partner to talk to Mr. Beecher? She lives in Ventura."

Dan shrugged. "Fine. But warn her. Howard's . . . different."

"Liz is used to people who are different," Tory assured him.

Letting his gaze slide lazily over Tory, Dan nodded. "Yes, I suppose she must be," he murmured.

Laughing nervously, Tory willed her body to stop responding to the uncanny heat of Dan's cool blue eyes. Her body, however, continued to have a will of its own. It didn't seem to understand that the man was indulging in a bit of mild teasing. All it knew was sudden, overwhelming desire. "We . . . we'd better go," she said in a small voice.

Dan didn't answer. He was transfixed by luminous amber eyes, parted lips, hardened nipples thrusting against thin silk.

The returning waiter broke the trance.

As Dan signed the receipt he told himself again that he had to stay away from Tory Chase. She was an enchantress. An enchanted man was a vulnerable man. He didn't choose to be vulnerable. "Thank you for giving me so much of your time, Miss Chase," he said politely.

"Thank you for all your helpful suggestions," she said just as politely.

As they left the restaurant, Dan was careful to resist the impulse to rest his hand on the inviting curve of the small of Tory's back. Touching her was out of the question.

But he couldn't block out the fantasy of whiling away the rest of the afternoon with Tory Chase in his bed and in his arms, her slender legs wrapped tightly around his hips as he lost himself in her sweet, tempting warmth.

Four

There was no distraction for a troubled mind like a dozen laughing five-year-olds with hand puppets and uninhibited imaginations, Tory mused as she let herself in to her office after a successful party.

There was also nothing more exhausting than keeping up with the energy levels of a dozen five-year-olds with hand puppets and uninhibited imaginations.

She plunked her basket of furry creatures on her desk, took a few moments to start up the coffee machine, then flopped down in her chair, leaning her head back and closing her eyes.

Dan Stewart immediately strolled into her mind as if he owned the place. "Get out of my head," Tory snapped, her eyes flying open. She picked up Cecil, fitted the puppet onto her hand, and turned her wrist so the rabbit was smiling sympathetically at her. "Cec, what's wrong with me?" she grumbled. "I'm twenty-five years old. Too mature to develop a crush—and on a client, of all things. I'm also much too happy with my life the way it is to mess it up with a stupid infatuation. Just because Dan Stewart doesn't fit the stereotype I'd slotted him into doesn't mean I should let him turn my brains to mush, does it?"

Cecil shook his head.

"I knew you'd agree with me," Tory said, then laughed at her own silliness.

The office door opened and Liz walked in. "Well, if it isn't our own Doctor Dolittle," she said cheerfully.

Sticking out her tongue at her partner, Tory snatched Cecil off her hand and tossed him into the wicker basket.

Liz grinned as she put down her briefcase. "You only talk to the animals when you're feeling a little crazy, kiddo, so I'm going to hazard a guess. You had another rendezvous with Dan Stewart."

"How do you know?" Tory blurted out, getting up to pour two cups of coffee.

"Elementary, my dear." Liz perched herself on the corner of Tory's desk and gratefully accepted the mug of steaming coffee Tory handed her. "To start with, there's a certain tension vibrating from you. A jumpiness. A hunted look about the eyes has taken the place of the self-satisfaction of a woman who's always been immune to man trouble." She sipped her coffee, then added, "Also, I was coming back from my morning meeting just about the time you drove off with your gorgeous client in that fabulous T-bird convertible of his. What a beaut!"

"Forget it, Liz," Tory said, only half joking. "Dan Stewart is my nemesis, not yours."

Liz cocked one brow knowingly. "I was talking about the car, Tory. The car. I'll bet you didn't even notice you were riding in a classic." Shaking her head, she sighed theatrically. "That's what comes of being brought up in faraway places with strange-sounding names. You have no appreciation for all-American institutions like those good old gas-guzzlers of yesteryear. Yet where would your own father have been without them?"

"Living in a brick house on Main Street somewhere and running a nice little hardware store instead of uprooting all of us to move from one oil company outpost to another every time his number came up for a transfer," Tory shot back.

"And there's the rub," Liz said.

Tory scowled. "Where's what rub?"

"Control. Keeping it. Being your own person and running your own life."

"How did your meeting this morning go?" Tory broke in.

Liz went along with the abrupt subject change. "Great. We have a huge retirement party to plan. Spare no expense."

"You and I are going to be a busy pair for the next while," Tory said. She reached into her purse for the card Dan had given her with Howard Beecher's address and phone number. "Could you pay a visit to a mad scientist in Ventura for the Stewart account?"

"Love to," Liz answered. "I've been crazy about mad scientists ever since I saw 'Son of Flubber' on TV."

"You're just plain crazy," Tory retorted with an affectionate grin.

Liz raised a delicate brow. "*I'm* crazy?"

"Sure. You want a second opinion?" Tory said. She picked up Cecil. "Is she crazy?"

Cecil nodded vigorously. "Definitely missing a carrot or two from the bunch," he answered.

Liz sighed. "You know, I feel sorry for Dan Stewart. He has no idea what he's let himself in for."

"Not a thing, Liz," Tory answered, returning

Cecil to the basket. "The man couldn't be less interested. Believe me. I have a sixth sense about these things."

Tory's sixth sense gave her no warning whatsoever when the phone rang on Friday night.

She was soaking in a bubble bath amid flickering candles and scented foam, a goblet of chilled chablis dangling in one hand, her head resting against a terry-cloth pillow. As she languidly reached out to take the call, she congratulated herself for having given in to the luxury of a bathroom extension. She was sure it had spared her living room carpet gallons of dripped water, considering how much she loved bubble baths.

"Miss Chase?" she heard as soon as she'd said hello.

Her pulse bolted forward and her hand shook, spilling cold wine on the slope of one breast. She let out a tiny yelp of shock.

"Miss Chase, is something wrong?"

Oh lord. Tory sank further down under the protective cover of the bubbles. It had been three days since her lunch with Dan Stewart. Three days of waging a losing battle against his invasion of her thoughts and dreams. Now he was joining her in her bath. "Why no, Mr. Stewart," she said brightly. "Nothing's wrong. Nothing at all."

Silence.

"Mr. Stewart?" she prompted.

"Have I caught you at a bad time?" he asked. "Are you . . . busy? I mean . . . if you have . . . company . . ."

"Not at all," Tory said, wondering if he was probing for information about her social life or simply being polite. She placed her bet on the latter. "Is there something I can do for you, Mr. Stewart?"

He cleared his throat. "I understand you're planning to go to Ventura tomorrow to meet Howard Beecher."

Tory didn't answer for a moment, distracted by the sensual impact of Dan's voice. Deep, quiet, textured with a hint of roughness, it seemed to float through the atmosphere and caress her slick skin like a bold, unseen hand. The man's dominating presence was so tangible, Tory could have sworn the raspberry fragrance of her bath oil had acquired an overtone of spice and citrus, and the moist air was so heavy with sultry promise, she couldn't breathe.

"Miss Chase, are you still there?"

His edge of impatience snapped Tory out of her erotic reverie. She tipped her wine goblet to her lips and drained it, then set the glass aside before answering. "Mr. Stewart, don't you think a man who visits a lady in her bath could let himself go enough to call her by her first name?" she couldn't resist saying.

Another long silence. Then, "You're having a bath."

"A bubble bath, to be precise."

"A . . ." He coughed. "A bubble bath."

"Mmm. Candlelight, wine, and perfumed bath beads. It's a lovely way to end a long, hard day. Have you ever tried it?"

Silence again. Finally, "No, no, I can't say that I have, Miss . . ." His voice trailed off into nothingness.

"Now, you were saying?" Tory asked.

"Saying? About what?"

Tory smiled. The imperturbable Daniel J. Stewart sounded perturbed. Good. It seemed only fair for her to be able to mess up his head a little, considering his habit of scrambling hers so badly she couldn't see straight.

But she had to search her mind to remember just what he *had* been saying. When she finally retrieved the information from her memory banks, she scowled at the phone. How did he know she was planning to go to Ventura? Liz had seen Howard Beecher only the night before, and it was just that morning that she'd told Tory she had to see the fascinating man and his wondrous inventions for herself.

Then she remembered. Roger. She'd mentioned the planned visit to him. He must have told Dan. "You have an efficient grapevine," she said at last.

"Yes. I do expect to drive down to Ventura tomorrow. My partner was so taken with your Mr. Beecher and his *Back to the Future* house and garage lab, she insisted I meet him. Actually, I think Liz is dazzled. Starry-eyed even, which is odd considering how difficult it is for any man to impress her. She's very attractive, so she's heard all the usual lines."

"I hope you're wrong about her interest in Howard Beecher," Dan said, sounding as if he'd recovered his usual poise. "Howard lives in his own world. I've never known him to give any woman a tumble. Five minutes after she left him he probably wouldn't recognize the lady if he smacked right into her—which he's perfectly capable of doing."

"You haven't seen Liz," Tory shot back.

"And you haven't met Howard," Dan countered. "But it's good of you to go there on a Saturday." After a moment's hesitation, he went on, "I've been meaning to drop in on Howard myself, so it occurred to me that there's no need for you to take your car. I could pick you up around ten. Agreed?"

"Fine," Tory heard herself answer despite her irritation at his peremptory tone.

"Good. Just let me check your home address." He read it off in clipped syllables, and Tory confirmed it. "Until ten tomorrow morning," he said.

"Ten," Tory repeated. "I'll be ready."

There was a long pause. Finally Dan spoke again, an intriguing hoarseness in his voice as he said, "Enjoy your bubble bath, Miss Chase." With a soft click, he was gone.

Tory sat up straight and replaced the receiver. She stared at it dreamily for a while. All at once she became aware of the wild syncopation of her heart and the excitement coursing through her, and she let out a groan, squeezed her eyes shut, and slid all the way under the bubbles as if a good ducking would clear away the nonsense in her head.

It didn't.

Five

Dan was almost surprised when Tory opened the door of her second-story apartment fully dressed. He'd spent such a long, sleepless night picturing her slender curves obscured by nothing but fragile, crystalline bubbles, he felt cheated to find her wearing clothes.

She was appealing, though. In her trim yellow slacks and a Hawaiian-print silk shirt knotted at the waist, she was as bright and pretty as a tropical garden.

Basking in her sunny smile, Dan surrendered to the inevitable. He gave up wondering what had possessed him the night before to call this woman with yet another lame excuse to see her and be close to her. As he gazed down into her heart-shaped face and sparkling eyes he stopped battling the mysterious power that seemed to have taken hold of him. He was bewitched. There was no point pretending otherwise—at least to himself. "Good morning, Miss Chase," he said, barely refraining from gathering her into his arms.

"Good morning, Mr. Stewart," she said with an

infectious smile. She stepped back to let him in to her apartment and shut the door behind him.

Moving past her, Dan breathed in the elusive scent of raspberries in the light floral bouquet wafting around her. His thoughts flew back to the vivid image of her in a tub overflowing with bubbles, her eyes reflecting the flickering candle flames, her skin awash in a pink-gold glow. He wondered if she tasted of raspberries. Wild raspberries. Small and sweet and juicy.

In an effort to cool the instant heat that sizzled through his body, Dan made a quick visual tour of the living room. White walls, tables, and bookshelves were brightened by bold floral fabrics on couches and chairs. Clusters of leafy plants, blooming flowers, and cacti filled every corner, a collection of carved tropical birds tucked among them looking so vivid and real he half expected to hear them squawk. The setting was perfect for Tory.

His gaze inched its way back to her, found her mouth, and lingered there to savor her slightly parted lips, tilted up at the corners, full and kissable. . . . "Nice place you have here," he said in a voice thick with desire.

Still reeling from the shock of seeing Dan Stewart dressed in casual white pants and a red polo shirt that showed his lean build to fantasy-inspiring advantage, Tory murmured, "Thanks. You too."

His dark brows drew together in a puzzled frown.

Realizing her words hadn't made any sense, Tory hastily amended them. "I mean, you . . . you're too kind." She looked over her shoulder as if checking out the room to see what Dan approved of. "Actually, some people think it's a jungle in there."

"That explains why I like it," Dan said, glad to hide his powerful feelings behind light banter. "I've always been partial to jungles."

"You couldn't have climbed so high on the corporate vine if you weren't," Tory commented. She reached into the hall closet for her handbag and slipped the strap over her shoulder.

Dan cocked his head to one side as if trying to pick up a distant sound. "Did you hear that?"

Taken aback, Tory stood very still and listened hard, scowling. "What?" she whispered after several moments.

"The familiar discordant note of Victoria Chase's cynicism," Dan said as he reached past Tory to open the door. "What did the corporate world ever do to you, Miss Chase? Except provide clients for your services, that is."

"I've told you, I'm a realist, not a cynic." Tory whisked past him into the apartment building's hallway. As his after-shave tantalized her senses, she wondered how Dan would react if she gave in to the urge to nuzzle her face into the hollow of his breastbone and rub her cheek against the silky coils of hair at the opening of his shirt. She supposed that kind of behavior wouldn't strike him as terribly professional. And she mustn't forget that her professionalism was what he was interested in.

Dan closed the door and stood to one side while Tory locked it, then touched his fingertips to the small of her back as they started down the hall toward the stairs.

Tory bolted ahead like a revved-up Corvette. Dan pulled his hand back and curled his fingers into a tight fist at his side. "You seem a little edgy, Miss Chase," he said, deliberately putting her on the defensive to distract her from the fact that at the moment the *J* in his name stood for *Jangled.*

Annoyed that she was so transparent, Tory nevertheless smiled and gave Dan the most innocent look she could muster. "Edgy? What gives you that idea?" Without waiting for a reply she added, "Maybe it's just that I'm eager to meet this wacky inventor of yours. Liz can't seem to stop talking about Howard Beecher. And she says he has a couple of robots I'm going to fall in love with."

"He has several, but I imagine she's talking about Stan and Ollie," Dan said. "They're the ones with the most personality."

Tory turned her head so Dan couldn't see the roll of her eyes. Trust him, she thought. Trust Dan Stewart to think walking computers could have personalities. "Who named the robots?" she asked. "Is Howard a Laurel and Hardy fan?"

"I am."

Tory's eyes widened. "*You?* You like Laurel and Hardy?"

Dan raised his brow. "Is there some reason I shouldn't?"

"No. No, of course not," Tory answered hastily. "So you named these little . . . electronic people?"

"Since I'm their godfather, so to speak, Howard gave me that privilege. But I gather that you're a trifle skeptical about Stan and Ollie." Don opened the stairwell door and stood back to let Tory go past him. "An interesting reaction from a woman who's been known to let a pink rabbit named Cecil do her talking from time to time."

Tory laughed. "Chalk up another touché for your side, Mr. Stewart. But I am not skeptical," she argued on the way down the stairs. "I just finished saying I'm eager to meet your electronic godsons and their creator."

"Let me get everything straight, then. You're

eager, not skeptical. A realist, not a cynic. You've also managed to sidestep my question about what makes you a realist about the corporate jungle."

Tory wondered why Dan was so single-minded about getting an answer. Did he take her remarks personally? She decided she had nothing to lose by being straightforward. "Okay, I guess I have to admit to an old grudge. My father worked for a multinational oil corporation for thirty years. Dad was dedicated, and Mom was the perfect company wife. They did everything they were supposed to—all the required socializing, the nose-to-the-grindstone weekends and nights, the transfers every couple of years. Then there was a merger and a corporate shake-up. Overnight Dad went from indispensable to in the way. He was given a golden handshake and half an hour to clean out his desk. He was fifty-two. Too young to retire, too old to start over—or so he thought."

They'd reached the main floor. Dan placed his hand firmly on the small of Tory's back to guide her across the lobby. She didn't jump. He didn't back off. "And you say you're not bitter?" he remarked quietly. "I think I'd be pretty resentful in the same situation."

She looked up at him and flashed a grin, her eyes suddenly twinkling. "As things turned out, that merger was the best thing that ever happened to our family. My dad took the lemon he'd been handed and turned it into tropical punch. He got together with four other turfed-out executives, formed an investment group they call the Over-the-Hill Gang, and in five years they've parlayed their savings and their early-retirement settlements into financial independence. Now nobody tells Dad where to live or what to do. He's his own man and he loves it, and Mom has a full-time husband instead of an occasional visitor. What's really great is that a few months ago the young turks who replaced Dad went running to him, grateful to pay for his high-priced consulting services when they found themselves up against hard times and had no idea how to cope."

"It just goes to show that a winner always finds a way to keep on winning," Dan commented as he opened the building's main door.

Tory swept past him. "It also goes to show that it's never too late to start being your own person—or too early, for that matter."

"So you'll work with corporations, but you don't want them to get a handle on you," Dan commented as he fell in step beside her again, cupping her elbow with his hand to steer her toward his car in the parking lot.

Determinedly ignoring the sparks Dan's every touch ignited, Tory lifted her shoulders in a shrug. "Who does?"

"Who does what?"

"Who wants a corporation—or anyone—to get a handle on them?"

"Some people are happy to exchange independence for security," Dan pointed out.

"For the illusion of security, you mean. But you're right. Some people are willing to make that particular bargain. I just don't happen to think it's a fair trade." Tory grinned at Dan. "Neither do you, Mr. Stewart. I've done my homework. I know you've been courted by the big guys. But you'd rather paddle your own canoe than hop onto a luxury liner with someone else at the helm. You're built to be captain, not crew."

Dan didn't respond. He remained quiet the rest of the way to his car.

By the time he was behind the wheel of the black vintage T-bird and Tory was buckled into the passenger seat, she was wondering if she'd offended him. "I wasn't taking potshots at Stewart Enterprises, you know. You're different. Your employees seem to be people, not numbers. You haven't lost sight of the human factor."

"I'm not so different," Dan said, slipping on a pair of sunglasses. "Keeping sight of the human factor can be difficult. Downright impossible, at times. You start with a lot of ideals, but you can't always hold on to them."

As he switched on the ignition, Tory studied him with new curiosity, suddenly realizing that Dan was wrestling with his own moral dilemmas, that he felt genuine concern about the strength of his own ideals and humanity.

"I decided to leave the car's top up," he said after a moment, as if reaching for anything, even the self-evident, to distract Tory from the glimpse he'd given her of his inner doubts. "There's been some construction on the highway for the past few days, so it'll be dusty. Do you mind?"

"Not at all," Tory answered, realizing she'd been staring at him, making him uncomfortable.

Once again a heavy silence descended as Tory began thinking about just what kind of pressure Dan Stewart was up against. A successful maverick was tolerated in his industry only so long before someone set out to absorb or destroy him. And if Dan cared about his employees as much as he seemed to, he was fighting to keep his company on top for their sakes as well as his own.

Dan was lost in his own thoughts, wondering if Tory Chase would feel anything but disdain for him if he finally had to knuckle under to the giant corporation that was wooing him with promises and threats, trying to get him to sell out and leave people like Howard Beecher to the not-so-tender mercies of their personnel department. Just why

Tory's opinion should matter so much, Dan didn't understand. He'd never concerned himself before with what anyone thought of him. But he did care what Tory thought.

And *that* was something to worry about.

Six

Less than a mile before the Ventura exit the traffic slowed, then ground to a complete stop. After several minutes a number of drivers started getting out of their cars, shaking their heads as they craned their necks to look at something down the road.

Dan switched off the ignition. "I'll go investigate," he said.

For the first time since she'd met Dan, Tory had a perfect opportunity to enjoy a long, leisurely look at him as he moved between the lines of cars.

She liked what she saw.

She envied the breeze that was ruffling his dark hair with invisible, irreverent fingers. The hard lines of his features were made to be memorized—and perhaps gentled—by a woman's touch. Her lips softened as she thought about trailing them along a taut cord of his throat to the hollow just above his collarbone, where her tongue could lap up an elixir of spice and lime. Her hands tingled with a primeval longing to know the silk coils of his chest hair, the ridges of muscle and sinew under his warm skin. His lean hips, taut flanks, and long legs conjured up visions that heated her blood to a slow, lazy simmer.

Drawing a ragged breath, Tory looked away from Dan. She'd gone too far. A heaviness had settled between her thighs, and her heart was pounding so hard, she was sure its erratic beat was audible.

But she couldn't keep her gaze from sweeping back to Dan. He'd stopped to talk to a small group of men who'd gathered to discuss the situation on the road. Standing with his hands shoved loosely into his pockets, he was nodding and saying comparatively little while the others seemed to be vying for the privilege of explaining the problem to him.

Tory was struck by his effortless aura of command. The men had sized him up, probably without being aware on a conscious level of what they were doing, and had accepted him instantly as the dominant male among them. The pecking-order rituals of the human animal were universal, Tory mused. She'd seen them in action countless times in innumerable settings. They differed only in detail from one culture to the next, one situation to another.

All at once her mouth felt parched. Her breathing grew labored as her throat seemed to close over. She told herself to stop being ridiculous. All that silly talk at her apartment about jungles must have sent her impressionable mind off on this primitive path. She had to drag it back to civilization before Dan returned, or she was liable to pounce on him like a lioness on the prowl for a mate.

She concentrated on taking deep, slow breaths, but almost choked when Dan turned and started back to the car before she'd had time to calm herself.

She was still gasping a little when Dan opened the door and slid behind the wheel. She hoped he wouldn't look at her, or if he did, wouldn't notice the state she was in.

"We won't be stuck here too long," he said. "A tandem dump truck jackknifed and spilled debris on the highway, but it's almost cleared awa . . ." He stopped and turned toward Tory. He took off his sunglasses with a slow, deliberate movement, placed them on the dash, and stared at her. He saw the flush spreading over her skin, the strange gaze in her eyes, the shallow rise and fall of her breasts. Galvanized by the sudden, electrifying eroticism radiating from her, he stretched his arm along the top of the seat and brushed the back of his fingers over her high, delicate cheekbone. Her skin was hot. A barely perceptible quiver shimmered through her, and there was a promise of captivating abandon in the way she closed her eyes.

Tory felt her grip on reality slipping. She was at the top of a long, slick water slide. If she let go, she would glide into a pool of pure sensuality, then float as aimlessly as a child's paper sailboat. Battling to hang on, she clutched at the only scrap of idle conversation she could think of. "Tell me about Howard Beecher," she virtually commanded, her voice strained. She managed to gentle her tone as she added, "You two seem to go back a long way."

"We do," Dan said, moving his hand to rest on the seat just behind Tory's head. Her soft hair grazed his thumb, her floral perfume mingled with her own elusive feminine musk to intoxicate him, and the swollen nubs of her breasts, straining against her blouse, were a secret invitation to his palm . . . his lips . . . his tongue.

Yet somehow he carried on as if unaware of the crackling undercurrents. "Howard Beecher took a chance on me when all I had to offer was a vague dream," he said, intently watching Tory. "Howard's garage was our corporate headquarters. Howard's mind was our chief asset."

"Along with your business acumen, your courage, your faith," she said with unexpected firmness—though she didn't look at Dan. She kept her eyes focused straight ahead. And there was an extra rasp in her husky voice, a breathlessness that undermined her white-knuckled self-discipline. "It seems to me you took as much of a chance on Howard as he did on you. But how did you two get together in the first place? From what I've been hearing about him, you're the ultimate odd couple."

"I suppose we are," Dan said absently, surprised by Tory's insistence on giving him as much credit as he always gave Howard for the company's success. She'd sounded almost protective. He shook his head slightly. Ridiculous, he thought. Tory Chase, all sixty-four inches of her, being protective of Dan Stewart? And Dan Stewart liking it, being pleased by her reaction? Utterly ridiculous. Yet an unfamiliar warmth stirred deep inside him. He fought it. The feeling could be addictive, could set up a need. He'd spent a lifetime keeping that kind of need at bay. He didn't plan to change now.

Realizing he hadn't answered Tory's question, Dan was silent a moment longer as he debated how many details to offer about the early days, when he and Howard had become friends. There was a danger in telling this woman too much. She would be too caring. Too compassionate. He didn't want her compassion. He wasn't sure just what he did want from Tory Chase—besides the alluring sweetness of her body—but compassion wasn't on his wish list. "Howard and I have known each other since we were kids," he said at last, his tone more curt than he'd intended. But he couldn't help it. He was under siege. "What brought you together with your partner?" he asked, deliberately putting the focus back on Tory so he could have a chance to regroup his defenses.

Tory wondered why Dan was so reluctant to talk about himself, but she respected his wishes. Despite the unsettled feeling his nearness caused, she somehow gave a calm recital of how she and Liz had met at the university in Los Angeles, worked together on event-organizing committees, and then decided to set up shop after spending a couple of years getting experience at established function-planning and public-relations firms in Los Angeles.

"So your independent streak doesn't rule out a partnership," Dan commented.

"My independence isn't a streak," Tory said, though with somewhat less conviction than usual. At the moment her independence felt like a fragile thread. "It defines me. It's what I am. And the partnership is a loose one. Liz has her accounts, I have mine. We share office space, help each other, and occasionally work together on a particularly complex project, but either of us could pull out at any time without doing harm to the other or to ourselves."

"So you always make sure you have a bolt-hole," Dan remarked, an inexplicable bite in his words.

Tory bristled, though she wasn't sure why. What he said was true. "If you want to put it that way, yes," she said with a defiant lift of her chin.

"I can't help wondering something, Miss Chase."

Tory suspected she wasn't going to like what he was wondering. Her chin went up even higher, and her brows arched imperiously. "Wondering what, Mr. Stewart?"

"How do you plan to deal with something that doesn't allow for easy escape hatches? Marriage, for instance. Having children. Or do you plan to avoid that sort of commitment forever?"

"I'm only twenty-five, Mr. Stewart. I have plenty of time. That decision is at least a few years off. I'm in no hurry to have to answer to someone, to follow somebody else's dreams instead of my own. I'll get there when I'm good and ready."

Dan slid his hand down from the seat back to cup the nape of her neck. "Your view of marriage seems to be even more bleak than your opinion of large corporations. By the way, what if the decision comes up before you're ready?" he asked softly, with no idea why he was pursuing an issue he normally skirted like quicksand.

Tory drew a sharp breath, but managed to answer, "It won't come up before I'm ready. I won't let it."

Reaching over to flip open the buckle on Tory's seat belt while exerting just enough pressure on the back of her neck to pull her toward him, Dan was pleasantly surprised to find that she offered no resistance. "You honestly believe it's possible to have that much control over what happens in your life, Miss Chase?" he asked with deceptive blandness.

"Don't you?" she countered shakily.

He reached up with his free hand to touch her lips, at first tracing their outline, then stroking the soft pink flesh lightly while he searched her eyes. "No," he answered after a long moment. "All of a sudden I'm beginning to doubt whether I have any control at all."

As Dan lowered his mouth to hers, his hand splaying over her arched throat, Tory resisted for mere seconds, then yielded with a shuddering sigh. Her arms crept around his neck and her lips parted with only a little coaxing of his tongue. He tasted, stroked, delved, and explored with ever-deepening possession as Tory gave whatever he demanded and offered more. His hand inched downward, skimming over the slope of her breast to cover one firm mound, the nipple thrusting into his palm like an eager kiss. She moaned softly, and Dan was enflamed by the helpless sound. "Tory, you're so sweet," he whispered against her mouth. "Sweet and warm and delicious, and I want you. . . ."

"Oh Dan," Tory cried, "I want—" Abruptly cutting off her words with a harsh intake of breath, she dropped her arms from around his neck and stiffened as if someone had hurled a bucketful of ice water on her. "Dear heaven, what are we *doing*?"

Dan took a moment to calm down, then removed his hand from her breast, placed three fingertips under her chin, and gently lifted to make her look at him. "Why are you fighting me so hard, Tory?" he asked, conveniently choosing to ignore the fact that he'd been fighting her until just moments before with every ounce of resistance he could scrape up.

Tory fell back on her usual ploy. "Fighting you?" she repeated, seemingly amazed by the very idea. But she couldn't back up her act this time. "I'm not . . . I mean, I'm just . . . that is . . ."

"Take a few deep breaths," Dan said in a wry drawl. "It's the best way to stop stammering."

"I'm not s . . . stammering," Tory protested. She opened her mouth to continue, but was saved by a cacophony of car horns and a trucker behind them yelling, "C'mon, T-bird, *move* it!"

Dan swore quietly as he saw that the cars ahead were rolling again. He released Tory, turning to put on his sunglasses and start the car while she shifted away from him and refastened her seat belt. Great timing, he thought, not sure whether he meant his own or the traffic's.

None of the silences he and Tory had endured in the past could compare with the tense quiet between them now. As the minutes passed, Dan began to have second thoughts. Perhaps it was just as well the road had cleared when it had, and even that the trucker had been impatient. Tory was right. What the hell had they been doing? What the hell had *he* been doing?" I apologize, Miss Chase," he said gruffly. "My behavior has been . . . unforgivable."

"No more than mine," Tory pointed out. She was sorry to hear the formality return to Dan's voice. A part of her regretted the wave of panic that had destroyed a blissful moment. Yet she was shocked, hardly believing she was capable of such a mindless response. No kiss should have that kind of power, she told herself. No man should be able to sweep away her defenses so easily and completely. No caress should sear her skin the way Dan's touch had.

And come to think of it, why had she let Dan put her on the defensive? She had a question of her own—the very one he had asked her. She decided to put it to him. "Mr. Stewart," she said tightly, "why are *you* fighting *me* so hard?"

He took so long to answer, she began to think he was ignoring her. But at last he said, "I'm not fighting you, Tory. I think I'm . . . I don't know. Shadowboxing, I guess."

Even more puzzled than before, Tory opened her

mouth to pursue the subject, then changed her mind and backed off. She had a phantom sparring partner of her own to deal with.

The tension became unbearable. When Dan finally wheeled the car onto the Ventura exit, Tory breathed a sigh of relief. "Is it far to Howard's place?" she asked a little too anxiously.

"No," Dan answered. "You'll be glad to know that our drive shouldn't last more than another five minutes, Miss Chase."

Tory clenched her jaw. Miss Chase again. Wonderful.

"We can look forward to a quick change of mood as soon as we're with Howard," Dan added, not sure why he felt the need to make Tory feel better about the day ahead. His compulsion to erase the little crease that had appeared in her forehead was as inexplicable as everything else he'd been feeling since she'd walked into his life.

Barely listening, Tory understood only after several moments what Dan was trying to do. She decided she ought to help. Brooding was childish. "What change in mood?" she asked with an effort to smile.

Dan didn't answer right away. He wasn't sure how to phrase his explanation. Finally he gave it a try. "This . . . this distraction between us . . . the way we can't seem to . . ." He sighed heavily, then summed it up as best he could. "Howard will be all business. He's so caught up in what he's doing, we'll probably catch his enthusiasm and stop . . ."

"Being distracted," Tory put in, suddenly glowering at him. She'd been overwhelmed by passion. He'd been distracted.

"Right," Dan said, grateful for her understanding. "Howard Beecher is the perfect antidote to . . ."

"Distractedness," Tory muttered.

Dan shot her a sharp glance. She sounded annoyed. But why? She was the one who'd called a halt to something that had promised to be very, very good. She was the one who'd frozen. "Anyway," he said lamely, "we can count on spending the next couple of hours in the most unromantic atmosphere imaginable—for which I'm sure you'll be grateful."

Tory managed another patently phony smile. "You can't imagine how grateful, Mr. Stewart. The last thing we want to deal with is the slightest hint of romance in the air."

"Agreed. So we're going to the right place," Dan said, knowing he was belaboring the point. What was it about Tory Chase that reduced him to babbling, anyway?

Moments later he pulled into a parking spot on the street in front of an unpretentious white stucco bungalow with a red-tile roof. "That's Howard's place with the open garage door," Dan said.

Tory saw Liz's car in the driveway.

Dan got out and strode around to the passenger side to hold the door for Tory. She was already out and closing it by the time he got there. "I know it's not a big thing to get out of a car all by yourself, but I get the feeling you work at showing your independence at every opportunity," he commented. "Are you trying to prove something to me or to yourself?"

"Neither," Tory said blithely. "It's the way I am. I don't need to prove it to anybody."

They started up the driveway. Halfway to the garage, Dan stopped in his tracks and pushed his sunglasses down his nose, peering into the small building as if doubting the evidence of his own eyes.

Following his gaze, Tory grinned. She wasn't surprised at all to see a man—undoubtedly Howard Beecher—locked in a torrid embrace with Liz Collins.

Then her grin faded. So much for spending a couple of hours in a safe, unromantic atmosphere.

Seven

"There's something you ought to know about me, Mr. Stewart," Tory said in a low voice as she and Dan stood frozen in the middle of Howard Beecher's driveway, not sure what to do next or where to look. "I *love* saying 'I told you so.' And I did mention something about my partner and your Mr. Beecher becoming an instant item, did I not?"

"You did," Dan admitted. "But I still don't believe it."

Tory grinned and waved her head in the direction of the glued-together couple in the garage. "What's this, then? Some kind of scientific experiment? If it is, I'm dying to know what hypothesis they're testing. Or are they trying out some kind of glue? A new mouth-to-mouth resuscitation technique, perhaps?"

Narrowing his eyes, Dan shot Tory a look of feigned menace. "One of these days, Miss Chase . . ."

"I know, I know. To the moon," she supplied out of the side of her mouth.

Dan blinked twice, slowly. "How can such a

petite female manage to sound so much like Ralph Kramden?"

"It's this low voice of mine," Tory answered offhandedly. "A permanent frog in my throat. And I practice my imitations diligently—for my puppet act, you understand."

"Is there no end to your talents, Miss Chase? You're amazing."

Tory rolled her eyes. "I know. And such *useful* talents they are too."

"I imagine there are a few children around who think they're pretty useful," Dan commented.

Tory smiled, accepting the remark as a compliment. "How long do you think we'll have to stand around before that clinch is over?" she asked, beginning to feel very uncomfortable.

"By the looks of things, we could be here all day," Dan answered, deciding he'd better take action before he gave in to the temptation to follow Howard's lead, throw caution to the wind, and haul Tory back into his arms for another long, thorough kiss.

He gave a little cough to announce their presence. It didn't work. He walked a bit closer to the garage entrance and tried an ostentatious clearing of his throat.

Liz and Howard finally came up for air, turning toward the driveway with glassy eyes. "Oh hi," Howard said without the least bit of embarrassment. Keeping one arm around Liz's shoulders as they walked out to greet their visitors, he smiled lovingly down at her. "That's Dan," he told her.

Liz nodded, smiling at Dan as she shook his hand, then returned her attention to Howard, gazing at him in rapt adoration.

Tory was transfixed by her partner, barely seeing Howard Beecher. Even though Liz's attraction to him had been obvious from the way she'd spoken of the man. Tory hadn't dreamed things had gone so far—and so quickly! Liz and Howard had made love. The signs were unmistakable, the special bond between them almost tangible. But Liz was every bit as wary of involvement as Tory herself, and she'd never been the adoring type. What did Howard have that made him so special?

Tory took a closer look at him. For the past few days she'd been too caught up in her distrusting response to Dan to give his researcher much thought.

She was floored. It wasn't as if she'd expected a nerd, she told herself. Liz wasn't caught up in how a man looked, but she wouldn't go for an out-and-out dweeb. Still, Tory had formed a vague mental image of a typical skinny, bespectacled, absent-minded professor.

Howard looked as if he'd be more at home on a surfboard than in front of a computer. He was a blond, well-built, golden-skinned, green-eyed California dream in khaki shorts and a crisply tailored sport shirt in a lighter shade of the same color.

Something else belatedly dawned on Tory. Liz, who always dressed to the nines if she was going to see a client or anyone remotely connected to a client, was wearing shorts as well. Short shorts. And a midriff-baring top. She looked fabulous. Sexy. Radiant. Her blue eyes seemed backlit. Even her skin and her shining blond hair seemed to have acquired a special luster.

The thought struck Tory that Howard and Liz would make beautiful babies together. And Howard was gazing at Liz as if he'd like to get started on the project as soon as possible.

Tory slowly moved forward, beads of perspiration breaking out on her brow and at the back of her neck, the cool breeze no match for the wave of heat sweeping over her. The atmosphere surrounding Howard and Liz was heavy with the precise brand of raw sensuality Tory herself was battling.

It was going to be a rough morning.

"So you're the other half of Happenings," Howard said, finally turning away from Liz long enough to favor Tory with a crooked grin.

Tory nodded and thrust out her hand. "I'm delighted to meet you, Mr. Beecher," she said with the formality that drove her crazy when Dan resorted to it. "I've heard a lot about you."

"Ditto, but let's skip the last-name bit, okay?" he said, then did proper introductions between Dan and Liz. The first hint Tory had that Howard was more off balance than he pretended was when he proceeded to introduce *her* to Liz.

Liz laughed indulgently. "Howie, Tory and I have met, remember?"

"Howie?" Dan repeated in a strangled voice, then quickly recovered his poise as he saw his friend's face turning scarlet. "I mean, Howard . . . I think Tory is looking forward to getting acquainted with Stan and Ollie, and whatever other nuts-and-bolts characters you have running around this place."

"That's right," Tory said with a bemused smile as she and Dan went into the garage. She liked the way he'd smoothed over the embarrassing moment. He was a quick-witted and gracious man even when he was in a state of mild shock. It was all she could do not to slip her arm around his waist and give him an affectionate hug.

"What do you say we start with some coffee?" Howard suggested.

"I'd love some," Tory said eagerly. Perhaps a good shot of caffeine was just what she needed.

Glancing around the garage she saw robots, gadgets, and strange-looking games everywhere.

"A lot of these things aren't in the product brochures," she commented.

Dan was pleased. Obviously she'd done her homework. "We have to introduce them gradually. Technology isn't the problem. It's knowing when the public is ready to buy. That's why our new lines are risky."

"But exciting," Tory said as Howard led the way through a side door into a large kitchen that seemed normal until she took a closer look. "What goes on here?" she asked, her eyes widening. "A course in Cooking 2000?"

"You won't have to wait until the turn of the century to have this kind of kitchen, at least in some form," Howard answered. "A lot of the appliances are nothing more than slight refinements on common ones already on the market." He picked up a remote control and pointed it toward a small robot in one corner of the room. "Take my coffeemaker, for instance."

The robot whirred into action, not only grinding and brewing fresh coffee but pouring it into mugs, adding cream and sugar according to push-bottom commands relayed by Howard, and finally scooting around the room serving it.

"Talk about taking the sting out of getting up in the morning," Tory said with a delighted laugh. "Does that little guy do the cleanup as well?" she added teasingly.

"Of course," Howard said, unaware that she was joking. "I just have to set up his equipment and supplies about once a week, and he takes it from there."

Tory shook her head in amazement and tried the coffee. It was delicious. "Well, you've certainly hooked me," she announced. "I *want* one."

"Precisely what we hope people will say about every number in our new line," Dan remarked.

Tory grinned, already starting to get ideas for the launch. "They will, Dan. We'll make sure of it."

He believed her. And her confidence and enthusiasm meant a great deal to him.

For the next couple of hours he stayed in the background and let Howard demonstrate the products they'd be presenting as well as the ones still in development.

Tory was like a kid let loose in a playground, avidly listening and learning.

The warmth Dan had felt earlier intensified and expanded, flowing through him like the Gulf Stream through the chilly waters of the Atlantic, melting ice floes of frozen emotion that had been part of him for as long as he could remember. As he watched the lights dancing in Tory's eyes and listened to the husky ripple of her laughter, he found himself wondering if the impossible was possible—if all his years of teaching himself not to feel anything too deeply had failed to stamp out every spark of genuine emotion.

He wasn't sure whether he hoped so, or hoped not.

"Dan, what we have to work with here is fabulous!" Tory said, turning to him with a huge smile.

He snapped to attention. He liked the way she'd said *we*, as if she felt they were in this thing together. And that smile of hers . . . that lilting voice . . . "Is anyone interested in lunch?" he asked, his tone strained by the sudden tightness in his throat.

"Why don't we go for a sail and have a barbecue on the boat?" Howard suggested.

"What a great idea," Liz said, beaming at him. Then she turned to Tory. "Howie has a beautiful big sailboat that he keeps at the Ventura Harbor marina. What do you say, Tory?"

Tory wasn't sure what to say. She loved sailing, but she knew it wasn't the prospect of an afternoon out on the water that was making her heart beat faster. It was the thought of spending a few more hours with Dan that excited her. Yet she hesitated. She didn't want to make Dan feel cornered into going along, and she suspected he was too polite to refuse if he saw her eagerness. "We didn't count on spending the whole day here," she answered carefully. "I'm not sure we really . . ."

"Do you have other plans?" Dan asked.

"Well no, but . . . don't you?"

He shook his head. "I'm all for taking Howard up on his offer. Believe me, it's a rare privilege to be invited aboard his baby. He keeps the *Moonstruck* pretty much to himself."

"Really?" Liz said with a surprised glance at Howard. "He took me out on her the very first evening we met."

Dan gave Howard a quizzical look, but a burble of laughter escaped Tory.

Howard simply grinned and winked at Liz before turning back to the others. "So it's settled. Just give me a minute to shut things down here so I won't come back to a 'Sorcerer's Apprentice' nightmare, and we can be on our way. We'll have to stop on the way for the barbecue fixings and something to drink."

"If we take both cars, I can pick up whatever we need," Dan offered. "Besides, Tory needs more suitable shoes."

Tory blinked. She hadn't thought about the fact that she was wearing heels.

"We'll do a quick shopping trip and meet you at the boat," Dan went on, then briefly discussed with Howard and Liz whether they should have steaks and wine or hamburgers and beer. They decided on hamburgers and beer while Tory stood listening in a daze, nodding absently when they sought her agreement.

A moment later she found herself heading back to Dan's Thunderbird, his hand cupped under her elbow as if to steer her in the right direction. It was just as well, she thought. She might not get there on her own. Everything had happened so fast, her head was spinning.

For that matter, she'd been off center all morning, despite her delight in Howard's inventions and innovations. Each time she'd stolen a peek at Dan she'd had trouble believing that she'd shared a passionate kiss with him only a little while before; that he had crushed her in his arms and caressed her body with bold intimacy; that he'd possessed her mouth so thoroughly, her lips still felt swollen hours later, tingling and aching for more of the same.

But Dan's expression had remained so impassive, she'd decided she'd better get through the remainder of the session with Howard as best she could, try to hold on to her dignity during the drive home with Dan, and spend the rest of the day doing a manic cleanup of all her closets and cupboards to work off her nervous energy.

Instead, she was going sailing. With Dan. Sharing a barbecue lunch with Dan. Shopping with him.

The last place she could have imagined ending up with Dan Stewart was at a mall, picking up beer and hamburger fixings.

Maybe it was all a dream.

As she got into the car Tory shrugged off her amazement and settled in to enjoy the day—or the dream, if that was what it was.

Either way, she was having the best day she could remember in a long time.

When they reached the mall Tory dashed into a department store, while Dan went for the groceries and beer, agreeing to meet back at the car.

She raced through the aisles picking up white canvas flats, white shorts, a yellow halter top, and a tote bag to hold the clothes she had on. When she'd paid for her purchases she changed into them in the store's dressing room.

Feeling strangely shy and exposed in her new outfit as she strode toward the Thunderbird, Tory hoped Dan was waiting behind the wheel.

But he was leaning against the rear fender, his gaze moving slowly over her as he watched her approach. He'd replaced his slacks with denim cutoffs.

Tory swallowed hard. The man had no mercy. Those lean hips, that taut waist, those gorgeous legs . . . Her spirits faltered as she wondered whether her own legs were passing muster. They were slim enough, she supposed, and she'd been told they were shapely. But men liked legs that went on forever. Hers didn't. How could they? She wasn't tall enough.

"You actually managed to buy shorts as well as the barbecue goodies?" she asked in a breathless voice. "I didn't think I took that long."

"You didn't," Dan said as he straightened up and went around the car to open the passenger door for Tory. "I keep some casual things in the trunk for pleasant emergencies like this one. I'm sorry you had to buy clothes for the afternoon, though. Would you let me—"

"Please, don't even suggest it," Tory interrupted.

"I needed these things anyway." She sat down on the car seat, then swung her legs inside in one smooth motion. "Besides, I got them on special and I've always loved a bargain."

Dan lingered beside her for a moment. "You look . . ." Unable to finish, he took a deep breath and let it out slowly as his glance raked over her in one quick, intense sweep. Finally he murmured, "Very nice," then hastily closed the door and strolled slowly around to his side of the car, thinking as hard and fast as he could about fishing, baseball, and tax accountants—anything to give his libido a chance to settle down.

Nothing worked. As he climbed in behind the wheel there was a tightness in his loins that demanded an immediate and impossible release. His heart was pounding as if he'd just finished a grueling decathlon. He gripped the wheel with shaking hands while his imagination glided over Tory's sleek legs, felt the tender skin of her inner thighs, the warmth between them. . . .

Sharply pulling his mind back to reality, Dan wondered why he hadn't moved the car so much as an inch. Then he realized he hadn't put it in gear. He hadn't even turned on the ignition.

It didn't seem like a good idea to drive when he was in such a deranged state, so he searched his mind for an excuse to delay going anywhere for another few minutes. As he stared straight ahead, an inspiration hit him. "I'd better clean the windows," he said in a hoarse voice. "They got pretty dusty on the highway."

Tory hadn't noticed much dust on the windows, but men who owned classic cars were notoriously persnickety. Besides, as Dan got out, went around to open the trunk, and took out a rag and a spray bottle, she was grateful for the chance to pull herself together. Never in her life had she known that the hair-roughened skin of a man's legs could be so tempting to her fingertips. That the muscular curve of his upper arm could be so erotic. That the underside of his clenched jaw could be such an alluring invitation to her lips and tongue.

His *clenched* jaw, she thought again. Was he, after all, as tense as she was? And for the same reason?

A tiny smile tugged at the corners of her mouth as she watched Dan squirt cleaning liquid on the right rear window, then scrub in vigorous circles until the glass squeaked a protest. He repeated the process on each window, leaving the front windshield on her side till last. That one got a fast lick and a polish, with a nonchalantly whistling Dan studying cloud formations in the sky while his hands worked by rote.

When he finally got back into the car he said, "That feels better . . . *looks* better. Looks much better, don't you think?"

Tory didn't mention the streak across her side of the windshield that hadn't been there before. "Much better," she agreed. The window-washing interlude had served its purpose. There was a chance now that she might be able to resist throwing Daniel J. Stewart down on the car seat and ravishing him in a Ventura mall parking lot.

"Okay," Dan said with excessive cheerfulness. "Now we can go."

An incredible thought struck Tory. Was it possible that Dan was *shy*?

No, she decided immediately, remembering the way he'd kissed her. He wasn't shy. But he was . . . something. Distracted? Disconcerted?

Right. And she was bewitched, bothered, and

bewildered, she chided herself, all at once impatient with her car-seat psychology.

She made up her mind to accept the afternoon for what it was—an enjoyable interlude shared by business colleagues, and nothing more.

Eight

When Tory and Dan arrived at the *Moonstruck* Howard and Liz were already aboard. They were standing on deck in another clinch.

Tory rolled her eyes. Trying not to think deliciously impure thoughts while spending the afternoon with Liz and Howard was like trying to kick a chocolate habit in a Hershey's tasting lab.

"I still can't believe what I'm seeing," Dan muttered.

"To tell the truth, neither can I," Tory admitted.

"I've watched women do everything but handstands to get Howard's attention. In fact, I seem to recall one extremely athletic beach bunny actually *doing* handstands. Also cartwheels and backward somersaults and this crazy double-jointed trick of putting her ankles behind her neck . . ." Dan stopped and cleared his throat. "Anyway, Howard didn't notice her."

"But you obviously did," Tory drawled before she could stop herself, then swore under her breath as Dan's eyebrows shot up. Great, she thought. She'd managed to sound jealous. Retroactively jealous, at that. "The name of this boat is prophetic," she said lightly. "Howard certainly does seem moonstruck. Perhaps he always knew he would fall hard if he ever fell at all."

"Perhaps," Dan agreed. He looked back at the couple on board and shook his head. "Let's get this show on the road," he said quietly to Tory, then raised his voice and directed it toward the deck. "Permission to come aboard, sir?"

Tory smiled at his dry, teasing tone and wondered how she could have judged Dan as humorless.

Breaking apart, Howard and Liz grinned sheepishly. "Permission granted," Howard said, smoothing his palm over one side of his hair.

They loaded the groceries and beer in a quick bucket-brigade manner. Then Dan went aboard and turned to offer his hand to Tory.

She was perfectly capable of stepping onto a sailboat without help, but she accepted Dan's gallantry and didn't mind a bit when he held on to her a moment longer than seemed necessary.

At least three times during cast off Dan brushed against her when she thought he could have avoided it. Of course, she wasn't trying very hard to stay out of his way as she pitched in with the launching chores.

"You're a good crew member," Dan commented at one point. "You seem to know what you're doing."

Tory had been noticing the same thing about him, but his praise made her glow with pleasure. "I always wanted to sail, but there wasn't an opportunity when I was little. All that moving around we did in our family discouraged owning something as cumbersome as a boat. So I took lessons while I was at UCLA and crewed in a few races," she explained. "What about you, Dan? Did you grow up knowing your way around boats like most Southern Californians?"

"I'm not from California originally," he answered. "I'm like you—I took lessons at college. The closest I ever got to a boat when I was a kid was when Howard and I built a raft with an old sheet for a sail and a broom handle for a mast. We were in our Huck Finn stage."

Overhearing Dan's comment, Howard laughed. "I remember that raft. We were going to take it to the Mississippi and run away from—"

"Unfortunately, we were in New Mexico at the time," Dan cut in, then without missing a beat asked Howard which way they would go to catch the best wind.

Tory wondered why Dan had stopped Howard in the middle of his sentence and changed the subject so abruptly, but soon she was too caught up in the delights of the afternoon to dwell on the matter.

The division of chores fell into place without much discussion. Dan took care of the barbecue. Tory and Liz put out the buns and other trimmings along with the deli salads, fruits, and cheeses he'd bought for their picnic afloat. The three of them took care of the cleanup afterward. Howard, meanwhile, guided his craft with easy expertise and a contagious smile of contentment.

Tory was sitting beside Dan at the bow with her knees drawn up to her chest and encircled by her arms, her face lifted to the sun, and her eyes closed, when Liz came forward from the cockpit. "Tory, I just thought of something. Unless I miss my bet, you haven't put on a drop of sunscreen."

Tory opened one eye. "I forgot."

"You always forget. It doesn't matter as a rule, because you don't spent that much time in the sun, but today it does matter. You're asking for a burn. Here." Liz thrust a plastic bottle of lotion toward Tory. "Better late than never."

With a sigh, Tory thanked Liz and accepted the bottle. She squeezed a bit of the lotion onto her fingertips and smoothed it over her face and throat.

"Make sure you do your nose, unless you want to try out for a stint as Santa's lead reindeer," Liz said, returning to her perch near Howard at the stern. "And maybe Dan can do your back."

Tory narrowed her eyes and made a silent vow to get Liz for that one. The woman was in love, so she wanted everybody else to be in the same addled state.

A sidelong peek at Dan made Tory feel better. He seemed to be asleep, so perhaps he hadn't heard Liz's outrageous suggestion. Do her back, indeed.

After a moment of gazing at Dan, Tory hastily averted her eyes. Sitting cross-legged next to her, resting against the low wall of the cabin, his arms folded behind his head and his eyes shut, he looked all too appealing. Relaxed. Unguarded. Almost boyish.

Tory began slathering the sunscreen over her legs in long, sweeping motions, then smoothed it onto one shoulder, trying not to wish it were Dan's hand gliding slowly and sensuously over her skin. She realized it wasn't doing any good at all to resist watching him. The image of his face and body had been imprinted too vividly on her imagination in that one brief peek at him, Her pulse was thrumming unevenly, a nucleus of erotic energy was gathering such power deep within her, she wondered how long she could contain it. Her mouth felt dry. She moistened her lips with her tongue as she applied the lotion to her other shoulder.

All at once, as if sensing that something had

changed, she let her glance inch its way toward Dan again.

Her heart leapt into her throat when she saw that he was watching her. "Liz is right," he said quietly, shifting to reach around her body with one hand extended, palm up. "You could get a bad burn."

"I know," she whispered. But Tory wasn't talking about what the sun could do to her. Dan's warm breath was fanning the sensitive skin just behind her ear, and the nearness of his body was sending electrical charges through every part of her. Mesmerized, she squeezed a mound of creamy lotion onto his waiting palm.

She held her breath and kept her gaze fixed straight ahead while Dan rubbed his hands together to warm the liquid and spread it over both palms.

As he began massaging the backs of her shoulders, Tory suppressed a soft groan of pleasure. Struggling to focus her mind on something besides Dan's touch, she concentrated on watching the boat's sleek hull pierce the rippling waves below, spewing up feathery sprays of white froth. Her hypnotic trance deepened.

"Your muscles are all knotted up," Dan murmured, moving his thumbs in small circles down both sides of her spine. "I wouldn't have thought of Tory Chase as a tense person."

"Oh, I have my moments," Tory said in a small voice.

"Don't we all," Dan said, wondering why he was tormenting himself so mercilessly. He'd covered every exposed inch of Tory's back with sunscreen, yet he couldn't seem to stop going over and over the same delectable territory. He kept wishing her halter top dipped all the way to her waist at the back instead of just to the bottom of her shoulder blades. He fantasized about tugging on the straps knotted at the back of her neck, pushing down the two triangles of the bodice, and kneading her breasts until the tips were standing at attention, drawn out as if seeking the moist heat of his mouth. He found himself trying to envision her nipples and aureoles. Were they pink and fragile, like miniature rosebuds? Or dark, like late summer berries?

Dan felt a strange vibration in his hands, as if a low-voltage current of electricity were surging into them. When Tory began to sway toward him, his whole body tightened with urgent need.

He knew he had to back off, if only because he and Tory weren't alone on the boat. With teeth-gritting effort, he found the resolve to pat her shoulders and move away from her. "That ought to do it," he said lightly, though the thickness in his voice was like a confession of his secret thoughts.

"Do you want some sunscreen for yourself?" Tory asked, sounding as if she were talking underwater.

Dan shook his head. "I'm okay, thanks," he fibbed. He was anything but okay. He was in virtual agony.

Tory glanced back and saw that Howard and Liz were talking and laughing together. "Maybe we should rejoin the others," she suggested.

"Good idea," Dan agreed. Safety in numbers.

They managed to get through the rest of their afternoon voyage without indulging in anything more volatile than a few meaningful gazes and supposedly accidental touches.

The *Moonstruck* raced the sunset back to the marina and made it just as the sky began darkening to the intense indigo of Dan's eyes.

Tory sighed as she helped pull in the sails. She

knew she'd just spent a very special day. A memorable day. A day that wasn't likely to be repeated—not with Dan, anyway. She'd accepted that he was physically drawn to her but determined not to get involved. Now he would drive her home, say good night at the door, and go back to his real life. Possibly to some woman he *was* involved with.

It was just as well, Tory told herself. Dan Stewart could break her heart. She had no defenses against him. He was the man she was supposed to be fending off with every ounce of willpower she could muster, and suddenly she couldn't muster any at all.

As they left the boat Tory smiled at Dan, then at Howard and Liz. "Thanks for today. I don't know when I've enjoyed anything as much as . . . as that sail."

"It was a good one," Howard agreed, draping his arm around Liz's shoulders.

Dan sensed Tory's bittersweet mood. He felt the same way. But he'd had some time to think since he'd lost his cool earlier. Nothing had changed. *He* hadn't changed. And neither had Tory. For all her brave talk of independence, for all her superficial avoidance of commitment, she was a vulnerable, soft, loving female who would give her all to a man she cared about. It would be so easy to appease his hunger for her, to enjoy her until he started running true to form—and started running, period. She deserved better. The kindest thing he could do for Tory would be to take her home, say good night at the door, and start thinking about finding a woman who didn't need a man she could count on.

They were walking past one of the outdoor restaurants on the pier when Howard suddenly said, "Hey, it's been a few hours since we had those burgers, and this is a great seafood place. Why don't we cap off a perfect day with a terrific evening?"

Bad idea, Dan thought. "Sounds good to me," he heard himself say.

Tory's heartbeat skidded to a stop. She knew she ought to tell Dan she would prefer to go home right away. Any excuse would do. Biting down on her lower lip as she saw her companions looking at her and waiting for her answer, she hesitated.

Finally she murmured helplessly, "I'd love some seafood."

Howard was right, Dan decided as they finished dinner and ordered coffee. The dockside restaurant was a great seafood place.

But Howard hadn't mentioned one detail—the patio for dancing. Slow dancing. Slow dancing under the stars to romantic, sexy music. Dan knew that dancing with Tory in that setting, to that music, would spell the end of all his noble intentions. Half-listening to Howard telling some childhood anecdote, he made up his mind to whisk Tory out of the place and drive her straight home as soon as they'd had their coffee.

Suddenly Howard caught Dan's full attention by returning to the story of the raft they'd built when they were youngsters.

"We were about ten," Howard said. "We both hated the foster homes we were living in at the time, so we decided to sail off into the sunset."

Tory looked sharply at Dan. "Foster homes?"

"Sure," Howard went on. "Didn't Dan tell you how we got to be friends in the first place? We were both orphans. Well, I was an orphan, anyway. Never knew my folks, or at least not so I'd remember, and I didn't have any relatives masochistic enough to take on the squalling brat I apparently was. Dan, on the other hand, was—"

"A precocious bachelor who left home very young," Dan cut in.

Howard and Liz laughed at his flippant comment, but Tory studied Dan intently. "How young?"

He shrugged. "Three."

"Dan hates the word *foundling*," Howard said, shaking his head and chuckling.

"I was the child of an unwed mother who tried to take care of me and couldn't manage it, so she left me with the minister of a church in Albuquerque," Dan recited in a resigned monotone. He admired Howard for being so forthright about the checkered background they shared, but he hadn't wanted to get into it with Tory. She was too tenderhearted. She would see it all as a real tearjerker. Already she was looking at him with those huge doe eyes of hers, all soft and sad as if she wanted to reach back in time and change the way things had been for him. He had to set her straight. "When I'd overstayed my welcome the minister got the local authorities to find a foster family to take me in. Howard was already there, and somehow we kept dogging each other's footsteps afterward. We didn't know it then, but we were luckier than most kids."

"Luckier than most kids?" Tory repeated. "Are you serious?"

"Absolutely," he said, determined to put his dreary little tale behind them and move on to something else. "We were forced to learn valuable lessons early. People skills, for instance. Temporary foster parents usually aren't as easy to con and lean on as permanent, real ones. And then there was the creativity. The self-reliance. We had to devise our own games and entertainment."

"Such as building a raft and trying to reach the Mississippi from New Mexico?" Tory said, dismayed to find herself blinking back tears.

"Okay, so geography wasn't our best subject," Howard said with a grin. "Anyway, we figured there had to be a tributary around somewhere."

"Doesn't every kid decide to run away from home at some point?" Dan asked, then looked at Tory. He wished he hadn't. She looked so stricken. She was on the verge of weeping. And he was on the verge of dragging her into his arms to comfort her. "Didn't you pull that kind of stunt?" he asked gruffly.

Realizing that Dan was uncomfortable, Tory silently chided herself for being so emotional. "Every single time we moved I decided to run away from home. I always wanted to go back to where we'd just been," she said with a smile, trying to give Dan a break by putting the spotlight on herself. "Once I actually did go, but mostly I backed down halfway through packing because I couldn't choose which of my dollies to take along and which to leave behind. I didn't want any of them to feel—" She stopped short, realizing with horror that she'd almost said she hadn't wanted them to feel abandoned. How could she be so insensitive?

Howard and Liz smiled as if they hadn't noticed Tory's gaffe.

But Dan noticed. He also noticed that Tory was upset, and he felt an almost painful tug at his heartstrings. She'd been deflecting the conversation for his sake, and now she was afraid she'd hurt him. She hadn't. He wasn't walking around with a chip on his shoulder. He'd gotten rid of that burden more than a decade ago. But the little girl who'd considered the feelings of her dolls obviously hadn't changed much. "What about the one time you didn't back down?" he prompted.

"I was afraid you'd ask," Tory said, though she was glad he'd encouraged her to go on. Maybe she didn't have to walk on eggs with him. "The oil company my father worked for had transferred him from Oklahoma to Canada. Calgary, Alberta, to be specific. I was about seven, and as usual I hated being the new kid in class. I wanted to go back to my old school and be with the friends I'd made there, so I told all my dolls they'd have to stay behind and take care of one another until I could send for them. I packed a peanut butter and jelly sandwich, a pair of pajamas, and my piggy bank. Then I crept out the back door of our house and ran until I couldn't run any more." She laughed and shook her head. "The jig was up when I flagged down a cab and asked the driver how many pennies it cost to get to Oklahoma. Geography wasn't my strong suit either. I was such a dope."

"You were only seven," Dan said heatedly, leaping to her defense. When Tory shot him a quizzical smile, he scowled and began pushing food around on his plate as he mumbled, "So what happened?"

"The driver told me to get into the cab, and when I did he quizzed me until he got my address," Tory answered, staring at Dan as she tried in vain to follow the workings of his mind. "By the time my rescuer had taken me back home he'd persuaded me to give Calgary another chance. He'd also promised to introduce me to his own little girl, who happened to be my age. And he followed through. His daughter became my new best friend, and to this day we keep in touch."

"A happy ending," Liz commented. "Things usually seem to work out that way for Tory."

Aware that Liz was watching him carefully as

she spoke, Dan's guard shot up like an invisible shield. "That incident could have turned out badly. Tory was fortunate."

"Or she brings out the best side of other people," Liz countered.

Dan looked at Tory as if mulling over that possibility, then gave his head a shake. "You're assuming there's always a best side in other people to be brought out, Liz. Sometimes there isn't."

Tory decided she'd been the center of attention long enough, so she jumped in with an overly enthusiastic change of subject. "One thing's certain. Somebody brought out the best in the chef this evening. This seafood plate is out of this world. Howard, as a food critic you've won my complete confidence."

The ploy worked. Howard, oblivious to the undercurrents at the table—or pretending not to notice them—chatted easily about other restaurants he liked until everyone was drawn into a lively discussion about the frantic trendiness of California cuisine.

Once again Tory found herself enjoying Dan's dry wit, his quietly ironic comments, his satirical descriptions of meals he'd been served in some of LA's most exclusive spots. "I like to think I'm open-minded, but I drew the line a long time ago at nibbling nasturtium petals," he said. He turned to Tory with a wink meant just for her. "I'd rather chow down an iguana steak."

Remembering their lunch at *Leapin' Lizards,* Tory laughed and somehow felt very special because he'd teased her.

"Uh-oh," Liz said, scraping back her chair and standing up. "I sense a private joke here. Howie, would you do me the honor? That's a Nat

King Cole song. It's sacrilegious not to dance to it."

Howard got to his feet and slid his arm around her waist as they headed for the dance floor.

"Liz is in for it now," Dan said. "Howard doesn't know a waltz from a widget."

Tory smiled. "Liz will teach him."

"He'll break all her toes."

"Care to bet on that, Mr. Stewart?"

Dan knew they were using banter to cover the awkwardness of the moment when he should have been asking Tory if she would like to dance. He was tempted to skip the chitchat, lead her onto the floor, and let Nat King Cole work his magic. But he kept telling himself it wouldn't be fair to carry on with a flirtation he'd started in a moment of weakness. "Miss Chase, I believe I'll pass on that wager," he said lightly. "You look too confident."

"I don't have your poker face," Tory said with an exaggerated sigh of disappointment. "Have you ever thought of being a professional gambler?"

"As a matter of fact, yes."

Tory's eyes widened. "You have? Really?"

"Really. For a couple of years when I was in my late teens professional gambling looked like my best option. I'd discovered there was no money in street fighting and cop baiting." Dan hesitated, then went on. "When I was still too young to be out on my own but too ornery to be welcome in a foster family, I was sent to a place euphemistically referred to as a home for troubled boys. It was there that I discovered I was pretty good at cards. By the time I was old enough to be accepted into some high-stakes games, I'd decided I was tired of fighting the world, so I used my ill-gotten gains to finance a decent education. Summer jobs as a dealer in Vegas helped. So you might say that my poker face earned me my MBA."

"Oh Dan," Tory murmured. "I'm so—"

"Stop right there," he said firmly. "I don't want any of that oh-Dan stuff, all right? I'm telling you these things because . . . because . . ." Frowning, he realized he had no idea why he was opening up to Tory. It wasn't like him. "Howard," he decided aloud. "Howard seems to be in a nostalgic mood tonight, maybe because of all the old songs they're playing. His openness must be catching."

Tory was beginning to piece together enough of a picture of Dan Stewart to understand him a little better—and to be more curious than ever about the missing parts of the puzzle. She had a dozen questions to ask him, but not one of them seemed to be any of her business. So she merely smiled and said, "By the way, I'm not sure which of us would have won my bet." She indicated the dance floor with a slight inclination of her head. "It depends on what you call dancing."

Dan followed her glance. He saw Howard and Liz glued together, swaying as one and occasionally taking a step in approximate time to the music. Howard's eyes were closed and his blissful smile seemed to be in place for life.

"Oh hell." Dan groaned, pushing back his chair and getting to his feet. "Let's dance, dammit."

Tory's knees went weak, but she managed to stand up and even smile sweetly. "Why, I'd love to. After all, how could I resist such a beautifully expressed invitation?"

Ignoring her gentle jibe, Dan led her to the dance floor as the music switched to a Sinatra classic. He pulled her close and bent his head so his lips were grazing the delicate outer rim of her ear. "Let me rephrase the invitation," he murmured. "Tory, would you dance with me?"

The sudden softness of her body, pliable and yielding in his arms, was all the answer he needed.

Nine

The song was Willie Nelson's version of "Stardust" and the sky had turned to black velvet studded with winking pinpoints of brilliant light. Tory didn't know whether she'd been dancing with Dan for minutes or hours. She only knew she wanted the night to go on forever.

At some point Dan had wrapped both arms around her waist, his hands loosely clasped just above the base of her spine. Her arms were twined around his neck as she rested her cheek against his shoulder, and her hips were swaying in rhythm with his.

As Willie crooned his last lazy phrases, Dan's arms tightened around Tory for a timeless moment before he relaxed his hold.

In a daze, Tory raised her head from his shoulder and languidly looked around. "Where is everybody?" she asked when she saw that she and Dan were alone on the floor.

"Gone," Dan said, sliding his hands up her back and curving them around her shoulders.

She blinked. "Gone?"

"If this were a marathon dance, we'd have won," Dan told her. "And I just noticed the waiters starting to make closing-up noises and breaking into the best guilt-inspiring yawns I've ever seen."

Tory looked around again. "What happened to Howard and Liz?"

"They left about five songs ago. Howard waved. Liz looked at him as if she'd never seen anything so clever."

Tory laughed softly. "There must be something in the air. I've never danced until closing time before."

"Neither have I. But maybe we'd better give these people a break and let them go home." Dan draped one arm around Tory's waist as they went back to their table. There was a note waiting for them. Dan picked it up and read it, "Didn't want to interrupt. Didn't want to be interrupted. Took care of the check. Drive home safely. H."

As she and Dan left the restaurant and strolled hand in hand toward the parking lot where they'd left the Thunderbird, Tory remarked, "Howard's a man of few words, at least at certain times."

"I guess so. I'm not sure I know who Howard is any more. I've never seen him behave the way he did today and tonight." It occurred to Dan that he didn't know himself anymore either, but he preferred not to delve into that subject at the moment. It seemed safer to go on talking about Howard. "Nobody ever called him Howie before. Not twice, anyway. For some reason he's never tolerated the nickname. But from Liz, it's all right. From Liz, it's music to his ears. I guess the old saw holds true—a man who doesn't fall easily takes a serious tumble when he finally does get tripped up."

"The same thing appears to be true for a woman," Tory said. "Liz has been a little batty ever since she met Howard. I didn't believe that sort of thing could happen to her. She seemed so . . . invincible."

Dan didn't comment.

Tory stole a sidelong glance at him and saw that his jaw was clenched again and he'd lapsed into troubled thought. She wondered if he'd realized the same thing she had—that they were describing themselves.

A shiver rippled through Tory as she faced the truth of her own vulnerability.

"Are you cold?" Dan asked immediately.

Far from it, Tory thought, but gave Dan an innocent smile. "The breeze has turned a bit chilly."

He released her hand and wrapped his arm around her shoulders until they reached the car, then opened the trunk and took out a denim jacket. "Here. Put this on."

"Do you keep a whole wardrobe in the trunk of this T-bird?" Tory asked with a soft giggle as she shoved her arms into the jacket's sleeves. "It's like a street mime's bottomless valise."

"You'd be surprised," Dan said, grasping her shoulders to turn her around. He zipped up the jacket, then looked down at her bare legs. "Maybe you should put your other clothes on. Your slacks, anyway. Are they in that tote bag of yours?"

"Yes, but I'm fine," Tory said. She had no desire to do a quick change in the parking lot or in the car. "I'm getting warm already." She looked down at herself and waggled her arms, shaking the several inches of sleeve that extended beyond her hands. "Your jacket probably covers more of me than my own things would anyway. But what about you?"

"I'm not cold," Dan said, opening the car door.

"If I were, there's a pullover in the bottomless trunk."

Tory climbed in, made herself comfortable on the soft leather seat, and suddenly realized how tired she was. She was covering a yawn as Dan slid behind the wheel. "Excuse me," she said, then yawned again. "I'm as bad as the waiters."

"Hey, it's late," Dan pointed out, turning on the ignition. "And all that sea air we breathed in today would make anyone sleepy."

"Did it make you sleepy?"

"No, but I'm tough."

"I have a feeling you're very tough. I certainly wouldn't want to tangle with you." Tory didn't notice her double meaning until the words were out.

"You wouldn't?" Dan said softly.

As Tory felt a blush creeping over her skin she hugged the jacket more tightly around her. She was tempted to blurt out the truth—that she would love to tangle with him, this very night or any other time he cared to name. But he shouldn't need to be told. Not at this point.

She changed the subject instead. Resting her head against the seat back and closing her eyes, she commented lazily, "This car is beautiful. Rides like a dream. But it seems odd for a man on the cutting edge of a future-world industry to choose a classic T-bird." She paused for several moments, then said, "I have a theory.'"

As Dan negotiated the car out of the parking lot he didn't respond to Tory's leading remark. His mind was on her conversational sidestep. He'd offered her the perfect opportunity to give him either a stop signal or a go light, and she'd left him guessing, talking instead about his car. She wanted him. That much he knew. And at some point during the evening his resolve to protect her from himself had evaporated like an ice cube tossed into a boiling kettle.

But he needed to know what she felt emotionally as well as physically. He needed to be sure that if she said yes to lovemaking, she'd made the choice when she was rational, not just in the heat of a sensual moment.

"Don't you want to hear my theory?" Tory piped up.

"Of course," Dan said, though he'd forgotten what she was talking about.

"The way I figure it, you saw a car just like this one when you were in your street-rebel stage," Tory ventured without lifting her head. She needed to keep chatting because she was getting sleepy, and the last thing she wanted to do was end the evening with a snooze. "You saw a shiny black T-bird and you felt like the proverbial kid pressing his nose against the window of a toy shop. You were on the outside looking in, and you didn't like being there. So you decided to get inside, and when you finally made it, you bought the one symbol of your success that meant anything to you."

Dan was astonished. "Howard told Liz, right? And she told you."

"Nope. I figured this one out all by myself." Tory grinned with unabashed satisfaction, her eyes still shut. "So I hit the nail on the head, did I?"

"You did. And now you think you're pretty smart," Dan said, experiencing another surge of the strange warmth Tory had a knack of stirring in him, a kind of warmth that had nothing to do with his desire for her. He liked knowing she'd been thinking about him, figuring out his motives for something as trivial as his choice of a car. He enjoyed her interest in *him*, not in his position or possessions. He loved the way she laughed at his one-liners as if he were Robin Williams and Billy Crystal and Steve Martin all rolled up in one, the way she listened to what he had to say as if he were the oracle of the century. She made him feel . . . valued. As a person. As a man. "Well, I've got news for you," he finally said, his voice scratchy with emotion.

"Hmm?" Tory murmured.

Dan glanced at her. She was fading fast. Reaching out to ruffle her hair affectionately, he said, "You *are* smart, Tory Chase."

She managed a drowsy smile, sighed, and slipped into her own world of dreams.

When Dan pulled up in front of Tory's building she was still asleep. Stopping the car, he debated whether to wake her or simply fish her keys from her purse, carry her up to her apartment, and tuck her into bed. He'd already made up his mind that making love to her on this particular night was out of the question. It would be like taking advantage of Sleeping Beauty. Besides, he had to leave for San Francisco in the morning, and at some point he'd realized he didn't want to spend the night with Tory until he could while away the next day with her as well. A leisurely breakfast. A long walk by the ocean. A bouquet of roses and perhaps a candlelight dinner.

That revelation alone was a sobering thought. Since when was Dan Stewart such a hearts-and-flowers romantic?

Before Dan could decide what to do about getting Tory upstairs, she opened her eyes and blinked several times. "Oh damn, I did go to sleep." She flopped her head to one side to face Dan. "I'm sorry. It wasn't fair of me to leave you to handle the driving without having some company."

Aroused against his will by a husky lilt in her voice that was even more pronounced than usual, Dan said a silent "down boy" to his libido and reached out to give Tory's nose a gentle tweak. "Don't worry. Your purring kept me company."

"Purring?" She bolted upright. "You mean I snored?"

"Would I use such an unfeminine word for your little . . . sighs?" Dan teased as he got out of the car.

Tory buried her face in her hands. "I'll never sleep again. Never in my whole life."

Dan opened the car door. "Come on, Miss Van Winkle. You're home."

With a rueful laugh, Tory shrugged off his jacket to leave it in the car—despite his protests that she should keep it on—and accepted his helping hand.

As she trudged beside him up to her apartment, she fretted about what to do when they got there. Asking him in for a nightcap or a cup of coffee would be so trite. Why not get straight to the point? If she wanted him in her bed—and she did—she should say so. What was the worst that could happen if she took the first step?

He might turn her down. That was the worst that could happen.

When they reached her door she unlocked and opened it. She was on the brink of suggesting a bracing espresso after all, when Dan took matters into his own hands. "Have I told you I have to head up to San Francisco tomorrow? I'll be gone until next weekend," he said as she turned to him.

Tory thought his voice sounded strained. And he wasn't making any moves to go into her apartment even though the door was open. She knew he was going to leave—and not for lack of desire. "You're so sweet," she murmured, swaying against him and resting her cheek on his shoulder, her hands curled into loose fists on his chest.

Dan instinctively slid his arms around her and kissed the top of her head. "I'm *sweet*? Why?" She'd caught him off guard. He'd been told a lot of things about himself. *Sweet* wasn't one of them. Had she somehow found out the reason for his trip?

Her answer surprised him. "You're sweet because you want to make love to me, and you know I want to make love to you," she said. "But you won't do anything about it because of my stupid fade-out. And because you'd have to leave early tomorrow morning. You're so protective, Dan. And so chivalrous. A gentleman in the real sense of the word—a gentle man." She snuggled against him and tilted her head so she could nuzzle his throat. "Could I have a nap right here? Just a little one. I'll bet it'd perk me up. Turn me into a real tiger."

Dan toyed with the possibility of scooping her up and carrying her to her bed. Nothing more. He would tuck her in, then leave.

Tory's body relaxed against his, and her breathing slowed. Good lord, he thought, she *was* having a nap.

He wondered if he could count on his self-control if he carried her to bed and climbed in beside her just to hold her. She wouldn't object. After all, she'd said she wanted him.

She'd also said he was sweet. Protective. Chivalrous. Dammit, why did she have to be so trusting? Why did she have to see a Lancelot when she looked at him?

"Tory," he said, "you have to go in now. You can't stand around in this hallway sleeping."

She gave a little start, then merely shifted her

tantalizing curves and snaked her arms around his neck. "One more minute," she murmured, her breath hot against the hollow of his throat. "Sixty seconds of shut-eye and I'll be ready to pop out of a cake or do an exotic dance, if that's what you want." She giggled and moved her hips in a sinuous circle as if to give Dan a preview.

He felt beads of perspiration breaking out on his forehead. He'd never ached for any woman the way he ached for Tory. And she was so willing. What was holding him back?

Easy question, he realized. Tory's sleepiness wasn't the problem; he had every confidence he could wake her up. The real issue was that she deserved more from a man than he was in the habit of offering. "Good night, Tory," he said firmly, grasping her shoulders and setting her away from him.

She wobbled and forced her eyes open. "Good night?"

"I'll call you when I get back."

Tory snapped awake enough to feel very foolish. "Whoops," she said, trying to make light of the awkward moment. "My seduction techniques seem to need a bit of work."

"Your seduction techniques are just fine," Dan said tightly. "But there's something you ought to think about before we take this . . . this flirtation . . . any further."

Tory blinked. Flirtation. Why did the word seem to suggest that everything she'd felt with Dan and believed he'd felt with her was trivial? "What should I think about, Dan?" she asked.

"That I'm not *sweet*!" he answered, suddenly agitated. "I'm a bastard, Tory, and I don't mean just in the literal sense. I'm the kind of man somebody should have warned you about."

Tory smiled. "I know that, silly."

It was Dan's turn to blink. "You do?"

"Of course. You're the kind of man every female is warned about the minute she becomes aware that boys aren't exactly like girls. I took that consideration under advisement before I decided I'd rather have one glorious night with you than spend the rest of my days regretting the fact that I didn't. But I do have a quarrel with you on one point, Dan Stewart. You most certainly *are* sweet. You're an absolute dear, whether you choose to think so or not."

"A dear," Dan repeated, shaking his head. "I'm sweet. I'm a dear. I'm a Knight of the Round Table. Tory, when it comes to men you're twenty-five going on fifteen."

She didn't take offense. She laughed. "Could be. And come to think of it, I'm probably much too inexperienced for you. So maybe my inopportune slumber was a blessing in disguise. . . ."

The rest of what she'd planned to say was lost in the hot recesses of Dan's mouth. Cupping one hand behind her head, he laced his fingers through her hair. The thumb of his other hand stroked a wildly throbbing cord of her throat. His tongue parted her lips with one aggressive thrust, then explored and tasted and moved rhythmically in and out as if to demonstrate the kind of intimacy he would like to share with her.

Tory was on fire when he finally raised his head and gazed down at her, his eyes searching hers. She was dizzy. She couldn't think. She had no will of her own.

"I trust we've put the question of inexperience to rest," he said, every word thick with passion. "But let me get this straight, Tory. You honestly do understand that I'm not . . ." He hesitated, uncertain what he actually wanted to say.

"Not a domesticated animal?" she suggested.

Dan frowned. "I guess that about covers it."

"See? I *do* understand," Tory said with a triumphant smile. Rising on her toes and cradling Dan's face between her palms, she gently kissed the furrows between his brows, the outer corners of his eyes, the tense creases bracketing his mouth. "You win, you lovely man. I'll spend the week giving sober second thought to whether I'm up to tangling with the likes of you, all right? Maybe by the time you get back I'll have come to my senses and decided to play it safe instead." She kissed his mouth, softly and affectionately, then sighed and moved away from him. "Good night, Dan. And thanks for a wonderful day," she said as she went into her apartment.

Dan experienced outright pain at letting her go—and at the awful possibility that she just might come to her senses while he was losing his.

She started to close the door, and Dan began walking slowly down the hall.

Suddenly she poked her head out. "Dan?"

He stopped and turned eagerly. "Yes?"

"I think I've finally figured out something."

He waited, one eyebrow raised, his heart racing. "What have you finally figured out?"

Tory gave him her sweetest smile. "The *J* in your name. It stands for Jughead, right?" She stuck out her tongue at him and disappeared.

Dan raked splayed fingers through his hair, wrestling with the urgent temptation to go back, pound on the door until she opened it, and make love to her all night long.

She was right. He was a jughead.

Ten

It didn't take Tory a week to realize Dan had done her a huge favor by giving her a chance to think things over. It didn't take her a day.

She got up late on Sunday morning, took one bleary-eyed look in the mirror, and saw what Dan had seen—a woman of twenty-five with the sophistication of a teenager when it came to matters of the heart. She was grateful to him for being so decent, but she was mortified. Good lord, she'd thrown herself at him!

"Must've been a virus floating around Ventura," she muttered. "Some kind of love bug." After all, Liz had been affected. And Howard. And maybe even Dan, for a little while.

For a *very* little while, she thought, glowering at herself. Dan had recovered in record time. Well, she would have a whole week to get her temperature back down to normal. Not seeing him was her best bet for a cure. After seven days without exposure, perhaps she could face him without risking a relapse.

But Tory hadn't counted on the complications

and secondary symptoms that could crop up in a week.

They started right away.

Her favorite FM station, for instance, launched a Weekend in 'Frisco contest, so every time Tory turned on the radio she heard Tony Bennett crooning about the place. She hated to admit that her own heart seemed to have wandered off in a northerly direction, or that Santa Barbara had lost its usual glow, but she was getting an inkling of how bleak her adopted hometown could be if it were littered with painful memories.

When she arrived at Stewart Enterprises on Wednesday afternoon for a meeting with Roger McCormick, Tory found her pulse kicking up a fuss for no reason except that the place was dominated by Dan's presence even when he *wasn't* present, and she knew she had a serious problem. The man hadn't just slipped past her emotional defenses, he'd razed them. Turned them into a useless pile of rubble.

Tory was shown into Roger's office immediately, for which she was thankful. Concentrating on work seemed to be the only real cure for what ailed her.

She sat down with Roger on his leather couch and placed sketches and notes on the table in front of him. After she'd finished outlining her rough plans, she said, "I wanted to get your okay before I checked out the feasibility with Howard."

Roger nodded. "I like it. All of it. But I think I ought to talk to Dan before I give you the go-ahead. You're suggesting quite a departure from the usual staidness of Stewart Electronics."

"I'm not sure there'll be time to put this whole thing together if we wait until next week to get started," Tory pointed out.

"No problem. Dan phoned an hour ago and left

a number where he could be reached all after-noon. I'll give him a call."

A surge of heat spiraled through Tory as Roger got up and went to the phone on his desk. She bit down on her lower lip and closed her eyes, silently swearing at herself for being so excited by the prospect of talking to Dan. But she couldn't help it. And surely she *would* be talking to him in a moment. He would ask Roger to put her on the line to explain her ideas, wouldn't he? He'd *want* to talk to her, wouldn't he?

She tried not to eavesdrop when Roger connected with Dan. She studied the watercolor sketches on the wall. She mentally rehearsed a summary of her plans so she wouldn't take up too much of Dan's time. She did everything but plug her ears with her index fingers and whistle "Dixie." Yet she heard every syllable Roger uttered and guessed at every word of Dan's—including the *no* he must have given as his answer when Roger asked him if he would like her to get on the line and explain things herself. He didn't even seem to want Roger to relay the gist of her ideas.

She was shocked. Crushed. She felt like marching over to Roger, grabbing the phone, and telling Dan she didn't want to talk to him anyway.

But when Roger hung up she merely asked, "What's the verdict?"

"It's a go," Roger answered.

"Super," Tory said, gathering up her papers. "Are you sure Mr. Stewart understood the details?" The details he couldn't be bothered about, she added under her breath.

"Dan was in a hurry," Roger answered. "All he said was that he trusts your judgment."

Tory snapped her briefcase shut and smiled as though posing for a toothpaste ad. "I'm flattered."

"You should be. Dan doesn't give blanket approval very often. He's a hands-on executive."

Don't I know it, Tory thought. Her skin tingled at the mere memory of his hands and what they could do to her. But a heavy weight seemed to be pressing down painfully on her chest. Dan had been in too much of a hurry to talk to her for even a few seconds. It was a coldhearted but effective way to let her know he wanted their relationship back on a purely professional footing. Damn, it hurt! But why? She wanted the same thing, didn't she? "I'll call Howard so he and I can set up a time to work out the details," she said pleasantly as Roger saw her to the door. "I won't be able to do any of the things I'm planning if he doesn't agree they're feasible."

"Howard's here today," Roger said. "He was in a meeting with his research assistants. I'm pretty sure it's over, though. Why don't I find out if he can see you right now?"

"That'd be great," Tory said, checking her watch. She had another appointment scheduled, but there was enough leeway to allow for a quick chat with Howard.

While Roger went back to his desk and phoned Howard's office, Tory gave herself a pep talk. She should be pleased that Dan had so much faith in her. There was no excuse for letting her personal feelings get out of hand. There was a job to be done for Stewart Enterprises. The more she concentrated on the work itself, the less she would dwell on the company's devastating president.

"Tory, Howard says he'll ice everything else to see you," Roger said, hanging up. "He's one floor down. I'll take you there."

"Terrific," Tory said, brightening her smile. "You know, Rog, I've never worked with such cooperative people. You and Howard really make my job easier." *Your president, however, is another kettle of . . . of barracuda!*

Minutes later Tory was in Howard's office being greeted like a long-lost friend, and when she'd explained her ideas his enthusiasm was a tonic. More determined than ever to keep her attention focused strictly on the project, she was careful not to talk to Howard about Dan. Any references she did have to make to Mr. Stewart were strictly professional. It didn't matter that Howard could give her some idea of what made Dan tick. She didn't want to know, any more than she would want to know what made a time bomb tick. All she wanted to do was stay a safe distance away.

Unfortunately, there wasn't much she could do about Howard's irrepressible openness or his chattiness—or his ingenuous enthusiasm about the fact that she and Dan seemed to have something special going. "Dan has never wanted to hurt anybody," Howard rattled on, much to Tory's dismay. "But he can't help it. You know how some women are, always falling for the guy who won't give them a tumble. Dan's like catnip to them. He's never been interested in staying with one person very long. But with you . . . I don't know. I get the feeling it's a whole different ball game. He really likes you, Tory. I just hope *you* aren't going to hurt *him.* You could, you know. You probably don't believe it, but I think you could do a real number on that guy."

"I wouldn't worry about it, Howard," Tory said lightly, struggling to ignore the turmoil of emotions Howard was creating with his confusing insights. "Dan and I understand each other. Now, about this project of yours to make Stan and Ollie talk like their namesakes," she said, steering Howard back to their plans.

To her relief, he didn't enlighten her any further about Dan.

It was while she and Howard were talking about programming the robots for voice commands that Tory tossed off a line in an Oliver Hardy impression that made him tip back his head and laugh delightedly. "Hey, you're talented," he said. "I think I could use you to help with the voice commands for these little guys."

She shrugged off the compliment. "I'd be happy to do what I can, Howard, but I'm not all that good. I just fool around with different voices so I can use them for my hand puppets."

"Hand puppets?"

"I occasionally do a little act for kids' parties," she explained.

Howard stared at her. "No kidding? You do? My gosh, this is too good to be true. Could I ask you to do me a big favor? And yourself, too, come to think of it. You can watch the robots in operation, interacting with other people—kids, mostly. And let's face it, if you can please children at a picnic these days, adults at a sales meeting should be a cinch, right?"

"Right, but what's the favor?"

Frowning and scratching his chin, Howard said, "I wonder why Liz didn't mention your puppets. . . ." He stopped and clapped his hand to his forehead. "Uh-oh. I forgot to tell her I needed somebody to fill in for the juggler who sprained his wrist. For that matter, I think I even forgot to tell her about the whole deal. I hope she won't be mad at me. . . ."

"Howard," Tory broke in, shaking her head in mock despair. "First, Liz doesn't get mad at anyone all that easily, much less at you. Second . . . what on earth are you going on about?"

When Tory left Howard's office a little while later

she was still assuring him she would love to show up with her puppets for the children's picnic he was coordinating for his service club the following Saturday afternoon. She wouldn't have to go far, because it was planned for the beach and park area on Santa Barbara's waterfront, a drive of perhaps ten minutes from her apartment. "And Howard, I'm a ham," she said over her shoulder as she strode down the carpeted hallway toward the elevator, rushing to go on to her next appointment. "I especially enjoy performing for youngsters, so quit thanking me. I'm flattered to be asked, okay?"

He grinned. "Okay. But thanks anyhow."

Tory laughed and pressed the elevator button. What she didn't tell Howard was that she was grateful to have something to do that would help keep her from daydreaming about what she'd been doing the previous Saturday.

Tory parked her car in a small lot on a side street as close as possible to the waterfront and walked the rest of the way to the picnic area. She carried only a yellow beach bag, leaving her puppets behind so she wouldn't have to cart the basket around until it was almost time for her to perform.

Spotting Howard playing Frisbee with a group of youngsters in the grassy park area above the beach, Tory went over to let him know she'd arrived. "You're early," he said, dropping out of the game to greet her. He gave her a quick once-over. "Is that a swimsuit?"

Tory nodded, sliding her sunglasses up to the top of her head. She'd worn a hot pink one-piece suit with a flowered sarong-style skirt knotted over it, partly so she could swim if she wanted to without going to a lot of fuss to change, and partly because she always found children responded best to her when she sported bright colors. "Would you like me to go down to the beach and keep an eye on the kids there?" she asked, knowing Howard would have a purely practical reason for commenting on her clothes. Otherwise he had eyes only for Liz.

"I'd appreciate it, Tory," he said with a grateful smile. "Liz has her hands full. Some of our other volunteers seem to be late."

"I'm on my way," Tory said. She pulled her sunglasses down over her eyes again and kicked off her sandals, dangling them from two fingers as she headed toward the water.

She and Liz had organized enough children's parties to have the drill down pat, so they quickly had everything under control and started to have fun themselves, splashing through the surf playing water volleyball and a string of other simple games with the youngsters.

When the volunteers arrived to help Liz, Tory stepped under the beach shower to rinse off the salt water, dried herself with a towel from her bag, and finger fluffed her hair. After she'd put on her skirt and shoes she began wandering the grounds, getting acquainted with the children she hadn't met.

She gathered from the organizers that most of the youngsters were from single-parent families and foster homes, and she liked the fact that Howard was trying to do his part to give the next generation what he'd never had. She was sure Dan would have been involved if he'd been in town—though it was hard to picture him coping with a bunch of lively kids.

Never mind Dan, she ordered herself, scowling.

She had to make him stop popping into her head. He was an unwelcome guest there.

"Miss," a freckle-faced boy of about six said, reaching up to touch her arm. "Miss, where's Deejay? Isn't he coming today?"

Tory's frown immediately turned to a smile for the youngster. She'd heard several children mention Deejay, but she knew nothing about him. Perhaps he was a disc jockey who was supposed to come and play music for them. "I'm afraid I have no idea," she admitted. "Who is this Deejay, anyway?"

The boy's expression suggested she must have been living on Mars. "You know, the clown."

"Oh. Well, I expect if Deejay is supposed to come, he'll be along soon," she said, hoping she was right.

Satisfied with her answer, the youngster scampered away to join the crowd gathering around Howard. Tory remembered the schedule she'd been given and realized it was time for Howard to start putting his robots through their paces. Liz had joined him, so Tory wandered over to stand with her partner to watch the show along with a gaggle of dripping children, fresh from their swim. By the time Howard was wrapping up his part of the program, Tory had been inspired with several more ideas for Dan's product launch.

She just couldn't stop thinking about that man, she thought with a sigh as she went to get her basket of puppets for her turn in the spotlight.

By the time she got back from the car she was pleased to see a clown surrounded by an excited circle of children. The famous Deejay had arrived. He was a good clown, too, she noted. His polka-dot costume was a riot of color, the Harpo Marx wig under his daisy-bedecked bowler hat an outrageous shade of lime green. And he hadn't cheated by wearing sneakers; his shoes were huge and floppy, the way a clown's shoes were supposed to be. They would make marvelous slapping noises when he walked.

Tory thought she'd like to speak to Deejay to find out whether he was a professional clown, not just a talented volunteer. Perhaps he would let her add him to the list of performers for Happenings parties.

Deejay had his back to her and was hunkering down to the level of the smaller children, so she negotiated her way around the ragged perimeter of the crowd surrounding him. She wanted to see whether his makeup was as spiffy as his costume.

When she finally reached a vantage point where she could take a good look without blocking a child's view, Tory found herself grinning her approval. Deejay had the most mournful face she'd ever seen in her life—an inverted horseshoe of a mouth, squiggly black furrows on his chalky forehead, large black-outlined teardrops etched on his white cheeks. He was twisting oblong balloons into the shapes of animals and handing them out to the youngsters, making sure he didn't miss the shy ones hanging back.

Tory wished she could move closer to hear his patter and get a better look at him. He was keeping the children alternately giggling and groaning with a sad-voiced delivery of what seemed to be knock-knock jokes, and when he plaintively asked if his audience could do better, they eagerly proved that they could.

Oh, yes, Tory decided. She had to try to get Deejay on her list of entertainers. He was special. He cared. These kids mattered to him.

When he'd given every child a balloon creature, Deejay straightened up and quickly scanned the group, obviously trying to make sure he hadn't overlooked anyone. Tory started to weave her way through the crowd to get to him before he left.

Just as she reached him, the gaze above his bulbous red nose met hers.

The startled, steel blue gaze.

Tory stopped dead, her heart leaping to her throat. "I don't believe it," she whispered.

"Where did you come from?" he demanded, looking like an absconding accountant bumping into his boss at the Air Jamaica ticket counter.

With a vague hand gesture, Tory indicated where she'd been standing. Deejay, she thought as she stared into the fathomless eyes. And that sad, sad face—who else could it be? "How ironic," she said softly. "I wanted to talk to you about working for Happenings."

Daniel J. Stewart lifted one thick grease-pencil brow. "Hold that thought, Miss Chase. If our new product line doesn't sell the way we've told the bankers it will, I may need the job."

"Not likely," Tory protested automatically, still stunned. "I've seen that product line. It's a winner. A big winner. Besides, as I understand it, the worst that could happen even if everything went wrong would be a takeover of Stewart Electronics by a giant corporation, with a plum position in it for you."

Dan shook his head. The daisy perched on his bowler hat jiggled playfully. "No thanks. I've heard about those giant corporations. Somebody whose opinion I respect once told me they run your life and then dump you just when you think you're coasting in for the finish."

Tory was surprised that Dan remembered the little tale of woe she'd told him about her father's experience. And she couldn't help being pleased by his comment that he respected her opinion, even if he wasn't being terribly serious. But she realized she was in even bigger trouble than she'd thought. Her knees had turned to guava jelly and the warmth of overwhelming sexual desire was flowing through her, and all for this . . . this clown! This clown who'd decided he didn't want her. This clown who'd refused to talk to her on the phone just days earlier.

"What are you doing here, Tory?" Dan asked after a long moment.

"Same as you," she answered, struggling for a nonchalant attitude. "I'm part of the entertainment."

"Liz must have spoken to Howard about your puppets."

"Actually, I mentioned them myself. Howard hadn't told Liz about this party. He'd forgotten." Suddenly a thought occurred to Tory. "And Howard didn't mention a word about Deejay to me."

Dan shrugged. "He probably forgot that too. Of course, I'd told him I wasn't sure I could get here, so he might have put Deejay out of his mind." Howard hadn't mentioned Tory's involvement, either, Dan mused. If he had, Deejay the Clown might have had an attack of paralyzing stage fright. Dan was glad he hadn't seen Tory in his audience until after he'd finished. Somehow when he'd dreamed all week of a reunion with her, he hadn't pictured it quite this way. "How did the robots behave?" he asked, struggling to keep up a normal conversation.

"They were perfect," Tory said. "The children loved them. Especially Stan and Ollie."

"Those two usually do steal the show. I wish I could have made it back in time to see Howard's latest refinements on them." Dan glanced down at the basket under Tory's arm. "What about your puppet act? Have you done it yet?"

Good lord, Tory thought. She'd forgotten all about her own performance. "I'm supposed to be on in five minutes. But how do I get my audience together?"

Dan looked around. "One of the volunteers seems to be rounding up the kids now. I'll go help." He started away, laboriously lifting one foot and putting it down carefully, then the other, as if walking on dry land in rubber flippers.

Pausing, he turned and caught Tory giggling. "Mind if I stick around and watch your routine?" he asked, ignoring her fit of mirth.

She pulled herself together. "Why would I mind?"

"No reason," he answered, then gazed at her for a long, charged moment. "But if I'd known you were on the scene when I was making those balloon animals, I think I'd have burst every last one of them."

As he turned and *slalloped* away, Tory smiled quizzically. Had Dan just admitted she made him nervous?

She pulled her loyal rabbit from the basket and tugged him onto her hand. "What do you think, Cecil?" she whispered, holding the puppet close to her face. "Was the man trying to tell me something? Did he give the teeniest hint of having some kind of personal feeling for me?"

Cecil thought it over for a moment, then shook his head vigorously. "Victoria Chase, when are you going to grow up?" he scolded. "Stop looking for messages nobody's sending. Daniel J. Stewart could have phoned you practically any night this past week, but he didn't. And he didn't want to talk to you when he had the chance. Get my drift?"

Tory glowered at the creature. "Cecil, go play in a foxhole, will you?" Suddenly deciding her lighthearted game of conversing with Cecil was going too far, she whipped him off her hand and replaced him with an electric blue brontosaurus she'd made the night before.

"What's that?" she heard.

Turning, she saw a little girl with blond pigtails and huge brown eyes studying the new hand puppet. "Allow me to introduce myself," Tory said in the John Wayne drawl she'd practiced while at the sewing machine concocting her latest creature. "Now listen up, pilgrim . . ."

Within moments she was surrounded by youngsters. Her show had begun, and she was in her element. She began to relax and enjoy the children.

She even brought Cecil out of his basket exile, ignoring the reproach she saw in his blue plastic eyes that said it wasn't always easy for a bunny to be Tory Chase's alter ego, chief confidant, and unofficial analyst.

Except for her constant awareness of Deejay in her audience, Tory hardly spared a thought for Dan Stewart.

Eleven

Dan was captivated. Enchanted. Rapidly losing the will to keep battling his feelings for Tory Chase.

She'd been on his mind practically every minute of the past week. On the day of Roger's call he'd wanted to climb right through the phone to reach her, or at least to get her on the line so he could hear the gentle lilt of her voice, the husky timbre that wouldn't stop haunting him. But it hadn't been necessary from a business standpoint to listen to her ideas, and he'd been telling himself so often to stay out of her life, he'd pretended automatically to be in a rush to get away.

He'd regretted the lost opportunity ever since.

Throughout the drive back to Santa Barbara he'd found himself getting excited at the thought of seeing Tory. But he'd kept fighting his eagerness. He'd depended on the children's party to keep him too busy to call Tory during the afternoon, and leave him too tired by the time it was over to phone her afterward.

But he might as well have surrendered from the

start, because when Tory had turned up in front of him looking so delectable in her exotic South Seas look, her lips parted and her breast tips stiffening visibly against the material of her swimsuit the instant she saw him, he'd surrendered to the inevitable. How could he do the decent thing when fate had thrown him such a tempting curve? How could he back off from a woman who looked at him with soft, moist, desire-filled eyes even when he was done up in clown makeup? How could he steel himself against her sweet sensuality, her irrepressible sense of fun, her playful charm?

He couldn't.

He stood watching Tory work her magic on the children, and on him. Not only was she funny and a delightful mimic, she brought out hidden talents in the young members of her audience. Encouraging the children to take turns working the puppets from her basket and playing let's pretend, she soon had even the timid ones performing songs, imitating their favorite cartoon characters, and playing out impromptu skits.

She finally brought her part of the entertainment to a close by having Cecil announce with an air of self-importance that it was time to return the rest of the puppets to the basket so everybody could race down to the beach for hot dogs and ice cream. The youngsters happily tore off, leaving Dan and Tory standing alone, smiling hesitantly at each other.

Now that she wasn't performing, Tory was tongue-tied. She hadn't expected to see Dan at this picnic. She hadn't expected to see him again at all—at least, not until the day of his sales meeting. And she definitely hadn't expected him to look at her with the promise of passion glinting darkly in his eyes.

Finally she spoke, her words hesitant. "I . . . I guess I'm all through here."

"So am I," Dan said quietly.

Tory bent to pick up her basket. "You really are a marvelous clown, Mr. Stewart."

"Thank you. By the way, Howard's the only person who knows I'm Deejay, and for all his openness he's never ratted on me—except perhaps to Liz. I have a feeling he tells her everything. And now you've seen through my disguise. The jig seems to be up."

"Not at all," Tory said with a ragged laugh. "If Liz knows, she won't tell, and your secret is safe with me."

"I know," Dan said quietly.

They gazed at each other for several moments more.

Tory broke the silence again. "The plans are moving right along for the launch. I think we'll make exactly the kind of splash you're hoping for."

"I expected nothing less, Tory. That's why I gave you carte blanche with this project."

"I thought it was because you didn't choose to talk to me," she said, then snapped her mouth shut. *I didn't say that,* she thought frantically. *Please. I couldn't have.*

Dan studied her with unnerving intensity before finally saying, "I have faith in your ability to make the right decisions, so I didn't need to hear details. What's more, I didn't want to hear them. I'd prefer to experience the impact of whatever it is you're going to do the way my customers will—without knowing ahead of time what to expect."

"Oh," Tory said in a small voice, properly chastened. But she felt much better about Dan's reason for not asking for her that day in Roger's office.

"But we both know I could have used Roger's call as an excuse to talk to you," Dan went on.

So much for feeling better, Tory thought, her spirits plummeting.

Dan saw Tory's crestfallen expression and couldn't help being glad she cared, but he didn't want to leave his remark hanging in the air between them. Yet he hesitated, not sure how to explain the unfamiliar feelings he'd been wrestling with, the crazy vacillating he'd done every time he'd been within reach of a telephone.

"O-kay, so now we all know where we stand," Tory said with a lift of her chin after several tense moments. She supposed she deserved the slap Dan had delivered, considering her sulky comment. But did the man have to be so honest? She made a bid to salvage her pride. "I really do appreciate your vote of confidence," she said with a forced smile. "And I won't let you down." She pivoted on one heel and started across the strip of lawn, forcing herself to walk normally when what she wanted to do was run as if she'd just heard the starting pistol in a fifty-yard dash.

"You just did," Dan said.

Tory stopped but didn't turn. "Just did what?"

"You just let me down, Tory. You didn't wait for me to finish. You did the same thing the first time we met. You're so quick to second-guess what I'm going to say and get your back up at me for saying it, even when I didn't say it and probably didn't even think it."

She turned slowly. "You wouldn't care to run that by me again, would you?"

Instead, Dan stomped toward her, his enormous shoes flopping up and down. "I'll walk you to your car," he muttered.

Staring at his feet, Tory choked back another helpless giggle.

Dan heard the little burbling sound and sent her a baleful glare. "Will you hang on a minute so I can change from these pancake flippers to regular shoes?"

"Why do you want me to stick around?" Tory said. "Do you need help?"

"I've needed help since the first day you walked into my office," he answered.

Tory's laughter died in her throat. "What do you mean?"

Dan lifted one black grease-pencil brow. "If you don't know what I mean, Miss Chase, you're even more naive than I thought."

"Even *more* naive? Well, Mr. Stewart, maybe I don't *care* what you mean," Tory shot back.

Dan heaved an impatient sigh. "Tory, I'm not going to stand here arguing with you. My feet are killing me."

She laughed. She couldn't help it. Dammit, she thought, the man could always disarm her with some quip.

As he stepped out of the clown shoes, he dug into the voluminous pockets of his costume for a pair of canvas loafers he'd stashed there.

"Don't tell me that getup is as bottomless as the trunk of your car," Tory commented, watching him. "Are you going to start pulling a whole outfit from your pockets like a magician's string of silk scarves?"

"Just the loafers," Dan said, removing his red plastic nose and pocketing it. He picked up the oversize shoes and carried them tucked under one arm as he rejoined her.

Tory thought Dan looked more ludicrous with his unpainted nose and ordinary footwear than he had in full costume, but she didn't want to laugh again. She was supposed to be annoyed with the man, not amused by him. "Come to think of it," she managed to say calmly, "you said I'd be surprised if I knew all the things you keep in the T-bird trunk. Would I have found this outfit if I'd peeked?"

"Not with just a peek. I make sure it's well hidden behind golf clubs and tennis rackets and all the usual macho stuff."

"And why do you keep a clown suit concealed in your car, Mr. Stewart?"

Dan lifted one shoulder in a self-conscious shrug. "To keep it handy."

"Makes sense," Tory said, nodding as if his answer really was an adequate explanation. "A high-powered electronics executive never knows when he's going to run into an emergency situation that calls for a clown suit." She shook her head and laughed, then said more seriously, "You were expected at this party, Deejay. The kids were waiting for you."

"Then it's a good thing I managed to get back. It was touch and go for a while. Heavy traffic on the coast highway."

"Where else do you perform?"

"Where else do *you* perform?" Dan countered.

"I asked you first."

"Okay, okay. Hospitals, fund-raisers, Christmas parties . . . you don't need the list. I'm sure I show up as Deejay in the same kinds of places where you haul out Cecil and company."

Tory shook her head in amazement. "Daniel J. Stewart, you're the Clark Kent of the Clarabell set. A closet clown. Do you change your clothes in phone booths?"

"No, I usually look for the nearest seltzer factory." Reaching the busy thoroughfare they had to cross, Dan cupped his hand under Tory's elbow and studiously ignored the curious glances he was getting.

Tory, realizing how strange the two of them looked as they hurried to the opposite side of the street, couldn't hold back another ripple of laughter. Yet at the same time she had to blink rapidly to stanch the flow of tears. There was so much more depth to Dan than she'd imagined—and so much more depth, as well, to her feelings for him.

Dan noticed Tory's strange emotional turbulence. "You're trembling," he said, frowning at her.

Tory didn't answer. Of course she was trembling. She was holding back a childish fit of hilarity because he looked so incongruous. She was struggling against an inexplicable weeping jag because he was such a touchingly wonderful person. She was battling the most primitive, insane, intense lust imaginable because he'd touched her. Trembling? It was a wonder she hadn't set off a minor earthquake the instant Dan's fingers had made contact with her elbow.

Dan didn't press the issue. They both remained silent the rest of the way to her car, where Tory put the puppet basket on the hood, then picked up Cecil, undid a zipper on the rabbit's back, and fished out her key ring.

"Clever," Dan commented.

"Cecil takes care of me in many ways," Tory said raggedly, returning the rabbit to the basket. She hesitated before trying to fit the car key into the door lock. She doubted her ability to manage it.

"How long has Cecil been on the job?" Dan asked.

"Only about three years. He's actually Cecil the Fourth. I was given his great-grandfather for my fifth birthday. I started telling all my troubles to Cecil the First and it got to be an unfortunate habit."

"But a charming talent," Dan said. He was

wondering why Tory hadn't opened her car yet. He hoped she was stalling, as reluctant to leave him as he was to say good-bye to her. "Do you really have to go right now?" he asked. "Wouldn't you like to stick around for a hot dog? I understand they're . . ." He tried to think of something special about the franks. "They're all beef," he finally said. Oh good, he thought disgustedly. Terrific. Now he was a wiener gourmet. How could any woman resist such a smooth operator?

Tory stared at him for several seconds, then collapsed against the car, burying her face in her hands as she made odd little choking sounds, her shoulders shaking.

"Tory, are you laughing or crying?" Dan said with sudden alarm. He had no idea what he'd done to cause such a reaction.

"I'm not sure," she answered, her words muffled. "It's just that you're so . . ." She shook her head, still covering her face with both her hands. "I never know what to *expect* from you!"

Dan dropped his clown shoes and reached up to curl his fingers around her wrists. "Funny, I was thinking the same about you," he said quietly, tugging her hands down from her face. "And just for the record, you're crying." Instinctively bending to kiss her tears away, he found his lips grazing over her cheeks and finding her mouth. In the next moment he was wrapping his arms around her slender body, crushing her against him.

Tory's hands searched for something to cling to and found Dan's shoulders, her fingers digging into his flesh. As her lips parted under his tender onslaught she was dimly aware of the odd taste and feel of greasepaint, but she didn't care. Her tongue met his tongue, stroking and dancing with uninhibited excitement, and the recesses of his mouth were sweet and hot and addictive.

"Tory," Dan murmured when he paused to catch a breath, nibbling gently on her full lips as his hands moved in restless circles over her back, bare almost to her waist. "Tory, why were you crying? Was it because of the things I said to you last week? Because I was fool enough to warn you that I'm not the kind of man you deserve?"

"I wasn't crying," she fibbed, her eyes remaining closed as Dan began showering soft kisses over her face. "And I don't care whether you're the kind of man I deserve, whatever that means. I was laughing . . . and maybe crying a little because you're so funny, and so kind, and so . . . so . . ."

"Sweet," Dan supplied, his voice low and intimate. "And dear. Let's not forget how sweet and dear I am."

Tory laughed again, tears streaming down her cheeks. "No, let's not forget it for a moment," she said softly.

Dan's mouth covered hers again. He slid his thumbs under the edges of her swimsuit and slowly trailed them upward to feather over the sides of her breasts. A soft moan of pleasure escaped her throat and her arms crept around his neck as her body arched to make it easier for his thumbs to inch their way to her taut, eager nipples, lightly circling and flicking them until she was gasping with need. He dipped down to nibble a teasing trail along the column of her throat, then traced the vee of her swimsuit with slow, searing kisses.

"Oh Dan, I want you so much," Tory whispered. "I've tried to fight it, I really have. But I can't. I just can't."

"And I can't fight wanting you," Dan confessed. "I've tried harder than you'll ever know." He took a deep, steadying breath, then straightened up and folded his arms around Tory, resting his cheek on the top of her head. "Things are getting a little out of control here," he said quietly. "We could get ourselves arrested if we keep on this way in a public place."

Tory sighed and nuzzled her face into his throat. They stood holding each other, struggling to calm down until Dan finally curled his fingers around her upper arms and put a few inches of space between their bodies. It wasn't easy. He was battling powerful forces.

He looked down at Tory and opened his mouth to speak.

Nothing came out. Suddenly an expression of horrified guilt swept over his features.

"What's wrong?" Tory asked, wondering if he'd heard a police siren and they really were going to be hauled into court for indecent behavior.

"Look what I've done to you!" Dan said, sounding even more stricken than he looked.

Tory was becoming alarmed. "What?"

"Your face . . . your bathing suit . . . even your *hair*! What the devil was I thinking of? How could I make such a mess and not realize it?"

Frowning, Tory looked down at herself and saw streaks of greasepaint on her swimsuit, her throat, and even the upper slopes of her breasts. She crouched to peer into the car's side mirror. Her whole face was smeared. There were smudges in her hair. Dan was right; she was a mess. A giggle escaped her, then turned into peals of laughter. "Hey Dan," she said between spasms of helpless mirth, "what's black and white and red all over? Me!"

"You're not upset," Dan said, astounded by Tory's reaction. He couldn't think of another woman he'd ever known who would consider it funny to find herself covered with secondhand clown makeup. He grinned. "You really aren't upset."

"Of course I'm not, silly," Tory said, straightening up. "And if you think I look bad, you should see what we did to your beautifully sad . . ." She stopped, her amusement fading abruptly. "Dan, you're smiling." Reaching up to touch her fingertips to his mouth, she murmured, "Right in the middle of the biggest, messiest frown I've ever seen, you're actually smiling."

"And you thought I was a hopeless case," he said quietly.

Tory nodded, her eyes filling with tears again.

Dan reached out and took her keys from her. "Let's get out of here. I don't have my car with me, so I'll drive yours while you concentrate on shutting off the waterworks."

"Good idea," Tory said, sniffling a little. "Where are we going?"

"My place, all right? It's within walking distance, and I have a big jar of cold cream for taking off greasepaint. I also have a chicken casserole in the freezer that could be even tastier than an all-beef hot dog." Dan put his hand on the small of Tory's back and steered her around to the passenger side, grabbing up his giant shoes and her basket of puppets on the way.

"You aren't comfortable with displays of emotion," Tory commented as Dan unlocked the door.

"It depends on the emotion. I was very comfortable with the one we displayed a couple of minutes ago."

"Quit hedging," Tory said as she climbed into the car. "You know what I mean."

Dan bent down to kiss the tip of her nose while simultaneously releasing the lock on the back door. "If you mean it kills me to see you cry, you're right. It does."

Tory opened her mouth, then closed it again. She had no comeback for that statement. While Dan deposited the basket of puppets and his shoes in the backseat and strode around to the driver's side, she sat very still.

Once again she was wondering if she really was with Dan or was having a lovely dream. Just in case, she didn't want to make a sound or a movement that might wake her up.

"Nice house," Tory remarked as Dan pulled into his driveway. The two words were the first she'd uttered during the few minutes it had taken to reach the modest bungalow with the ivory stucco exterior, terra-cotta roof, and well-groomed yard.

"It suits me," Dan said, switching off the ignition and looking at his home. Suddenly seeing it through Tory's eyes, he found himself adding almost apologetically, "Ordinary, though. Nothing special."

Tory grinned. "It's very special. Ostentation just isn't your style. And I happen to like your style."

He studied her for a long moment. She meant it, he thought with some surprise. She wasn't being polite. "I'm pretty impressed with yours too," he said gruffly as he turned to get out of the car.

He was walking around the car when a startling thought struck him: Tory was the first woman he'd ever brought to his home. And he'd done it without a second thought, as if having her there was perfectly natural. What was it about her that made him lower the drawbridge of his private self?

Dan remained distracted as he held the car door for Tory, then led her into the house. He was a little hesitant about what to do once they were inside. Making love seemed to be the general idea, and this time he wasn't going to back off. But dinner was on the agenda as well, and there was the greasepaint to deal with. He wasn't sure of the etiquette of the situation. Was there a macho way for a man to suggest putting romance on hold while he took off his makeup and put a casserole in the oven?

Making a quick decision, he took Tory straight to the guest bathroom. "The cold cream's in my bedroom," he said. "I'll get it."

In his room he took a moment to peel down to the cutoffs and tank top he'd worn under his clown suit. As he pulled off his green wig he heard Tory's husky ripple of laughter from down the hall and knew she must be looking at herself in the mirror. Another grin tugged at his own lips. All of a sudden his house seemed brighter. Cozier. Full of life as never before. He relaxed a little. Everything was going to be fine.

He found the cold cream and took it back to Tory. She was standing at the Spanish-tile vanity scrubbing one cheek with a dry tissue. "Don't try to do it that way," he scolded, twisting the cap off the jar. "Turn around to face me."

Smiling, Tory obeyed. Tiny copper flames flared in the depths of her eyes as she looked at him, her gaze moving slowly over his body.

Dan smiled back at her. He liked the way her expression could be innocent and lascivious at the same time. He liked the way she raised her face to him and stood passively, trustingly, locking her gaze with his while he set the jar on the vanity. He scooped out a mound of cream and began daubing it with the fingers of both hands onto her cheeks and forehead. He liked everything about Tory Chase—at least, everything he'd discovered so far. And he hoped to discover a great deal more before too long.

"I like this cream," Tory said. "It's almond scented."

"I'm glad you approve," Dan said.

Her gaze went to his lips. "You have a wonderful smile, Dan Stewart," she murmured. "I can't wait to see it when it's not surrounded by that huge frown."

"Maybe you never will," he teased as he reached for several tissues to wipe away the greasepaint-streaked cream on her face. "Maybe the frown is real and the smile is makeup."

She laughed. "Let's find out." As soon as Dan had finished cleaning her face and had tossed the used tissues into the wastebasket, she dipped her fingers into the jar and gently slathered cream over the garish red of Dan's sad clown mouth. "Lookin' good," she commented when she tissued away the frown.

Dan rested his hands on Tory's waist and let her remove all the remaining vestiges of Deejay. He couldn't decide what he enjoyed more—fussing over Tory, or being fussed over by her.

"Just as I thought," she said at last. She wiped her hands on a fresh tissue, discarded it, then reached up with tentative fingers to the outline of Dan's lips. "That smile is real."

Dan hadn't realized he was still smiling. He wasn't surprised, though. He was ridiculously happy.

"You know," Tory said with a playful gleam in her eyes, "you clean up rather nicely."

"I wish I could say the same for you," Dan countered.

Tory's lower lip jutted forward in a pout. "You beast!"

Dan laughed quietly, dipping two fingers into the jar of cream. "It's just that I missed a few places on you. Your hair, for instance. But there's not much I can do about the smudges there, except . . ." His voice became an intimate caress. "Perhaps . . . in a shower . . . later." As he spoke, he smeared the cream onto Tory's throat and further down, a few inches below her collar bone. "But here . . . Now, this is an area I can work on."

He watched the amber of Tory's eyes darken to burnished bronze. Her breathing grew shallow and irregular. As his fingertips moved in small circles just above the slope of her breasts he could feel her heartbeat accelerating. After he'd tissued away the cream, he hooked his thumbs under her swimsuit straps and tugged gently. "I should have done this sooner," he said. "It's sheer luck that I didn't get a stain on the cloth."

Tory thought he should have done it sooner too. About a week sooner. But she said nothing. She drew a long, shuddering breath and remained silent, watching him. She wanted to burn every detail of this moment into her memory.

Very slowly, Dan drew her straps down her arms, inch by inch peeling away the fabric cradling her breasts. "Beautiful," he said on a sharp intake of breath. "Tory, you're so lovely." Bending down, he brushed his cheek over each rose-tipped peak in turn, then his lips, his touch light and fleeting. He straightened up and smiled at her again. "You're everything I'd imagined, Tory. Everything and more."

As a quiver of excitement rippled through her, Tory started to reach out to Dan but found that her bodice, pushed all the way down to her waist, had imprisoned her wrists at her sides. She instinctively did a little shimmy to work her hands through the scrunched-up arm openings.

Dan let out a low grown as he watched Tory's innocently provocative movement, and when she began tugging his tank top from the waistband of his cutoffs he wondered whether he was going to have enough self-restraint to make love to her the way he wanted to. "Careful," he warned as he caught her hands and held them still, his voice thick with a sudden surge of need. "I'm liable to lose control, Tory."

"That's okay," she said softly, smiling up at him. "I can't think of anything I'd like better than for you to lose control."

"But not yet," Dan said. "There's so much pleasure to be had first." He gazed at her for a long moment, then stripped off his shirt and reached for her, resting his palms on her sides just above her waist, his fingers spread over her back and his thumbs grazing the undersides of her breasts.

"Amazing," Tory said, exploring Dan's sleek contours with both her hands.

"What's amazing?" he asked, a sudden hoarseness in his voice as Tory's palms lightly circled his hardening nipples.

"You look exactly the way I pictured you on that very first day. . . ." Realizing too late what she was confessing, she stopped abruptly and felt the blood rush to her cheeks.

"You too?" Dan said, smiling.

Tory's eyes widened. "You mean you . . . you were entertaining thoughts that were . . ." She laughed. "Less than businesslike?"

He drew her a little closer. "I wanted you from the moment you walked into my office, Tory."

"I had no idea," she murmured, sliding her arms around his neck. She realized that Dan hadn't lost control at all. He wasn't crushing her against him, but holding her so the tips of her breasts barely touched his chest. Tantalized into moving slightly from side to side, she closed her eyes and focused on the sensation of skin brushing skin, warm and textured and stimulating to all her nerve endings. She felt Dan's mouth graze hers, his tongue coaxing her lips apart, his fingers pressing into her flesh and drawing her harder against him.

"Lord, Tory, you're so soft," he said as he teased her mouth with gentle nips and brief forays that made her crave so much more. His hands began moving over her back, molding her curves to his body. "So soft and pliant."

Tory was reeling with pleasure when Dan trailed his lips down to her throat. His tongue dipped into a hollow just above her collarbone and found a throbbing pulse point. He licked at the spot, then nibbled his way up to her ear and whispered, "Tasting you is like plucking one of those spiky little mauve petals from clover and discovering the cache of nectar at the base. Even when you know it's there, it's a sweet surprise to find it." His warm breath tickled Tory's ear, making her quiver with delight. "And I intend to savor every drop," he added, bending to trail his lips over her throat and the slope of her breast.

After what seemed like a breathless eternity to Tory, Dan took one of her swollen nipples into his mouth. His tongue circled the aureole and flicked back and forth over the thrusting tip. Then he suckled as delicately as if drawing the nectar from a tiny petal.

A helpless moan escaped Tory as Dan gave both her breasts equal, loving attention. Her legs were shaking, threatening to give out completely. She clutched his shoulders, her head thrown back, her spine arched.

His hand went to the tie at the side of her skirt and seconds later the sarong was drifting to the floor. He covered her midriff with kisses while hooking the fingers of both hands under her swimsuit and pushing it farther down, his lips following in its wake. When it dropped to the floor Tory stepped out of it, as well as her shoes, and she was totally, beautifully naked. Dan lifted her as if she were weightless, perched her on the edge of the vanity, and stood between her thighs, cradling her face between his palms as he took her mouth with deep, untrammeled possessiveness.

Tory's hands slid upward from his shoulders until her fingers were plunging into his silky dark hair. Her legs curled around his waist and she pressed herself against him, the tiles of the vanity cool against her skin, Dan's denim cutoffs rough against her thighs.

"Wonderful," he murmured. He slid his arms around her and cupped her bottom with his two hands. "Perfect. I feel as if I've just been wrapped in pure silk. Now, just hold on to me. I want you in my bed, Tory. Not here." With a teasing grin he added, "Not this time, anyway."

His words sent tingles of erotic anticipation through her. Smiling at him, her eyes glazed with urgent desire, she tightened the grip of her legs and twined her arms around his neck. She felt the play of muscle rippling against her thighs as he carried her toward his bedroom, the flat plane of his belly pressed against the very center of her femininity. She was aware only vaguely of her surroundings when Dan stopped, brushed his lips over hers, and lowered her to his bed.

Tory was reluctant to let go of him, but she finally relaxed the hold of her arms and legs, lying back on the pillows to watch him as he stripped off his clothes. "At last," she said with a heavy-lidded smile. "But so worth waiting for."

"Tory," he said, stretching out beside her, "that special way you have of looking at me . . ." His remaining words were lost as she drew him down to capture his mouth with hers.

They began exploring each other, Dan gliding one hand over Tory's body, learning all the sensuous hills and valleys, lingering wherever his touch quickened her breathing; Tory's hands moving through their own tour of discovery, her fingers inching down his chest and stomach, teasing their way along a hipbone, the crease of a thigh, at last feathering along the hot, silken steel of him.

"Tory," he said with a groan. "I can't take much more of this. Wait . . . wait just a little . . . let me make you ready for me."

"Oh Dan, I'm ready now," she said with soft urgency. "I don't want to wait. Please, Dan. I need you."

"And I need you, Tory," he murmured. "But I want to make everything perfect for you, take care of you in every way . . ."

"You will," she whispered, her mouth moving over his face and throat and chest, leaving a trail of fire.

Prodded into surrender, Dan moved over her. As her thighs parted for him, he slipped one hand between their bodies and touched her most sensitive spot. She was ready for him. But moments later she was exquisitely ready for him.

When Dan eased himself into her, Tory exploded immediately in tiny spasms of pleasure and sheathed him in moist warmth, and all at once she felt as if her whole life had brought her to this one perfect moment, this sense of rightness she'd never even dreamed of.

Dan slid his arms under her hips to cup her bottom and lift her to him. As if reading her thoughts, he said gently, "Whatever is happening, Tory, let's flow with it. Let's not fight it. Let's just see where it takes us."

His gaze remained locked on hers as he thrust powerfully into her.

Her eyes widened with surprise that she could be penetrated so deeply, and that it would feel so wonderful. "Yes," she whispered when her body had adjusted itself to the welcome invasion. Filled by him, she wanted to go on forever feeling his movements within her. "Oh, yes. Again. Yes, please, again."

Dan's arms tightened around her as she took all of him. Hearts pounding, they clutched each other and rode the white water of their erotic rapids right to the brink of a cataract, remained poised there for a timeless moment, then cascaded over the precipice to drift down into a tranquil pool below.

Floating in Dan's arms, Tory knew she would never regret the moments she'd just shared with him. Even if his words of a week before had been meant to prepare her for an emotional withdrawal, this time together would make any future heartache easier to bear.

Twelve

"Your hair's a mess," Dan commented as he cuddled Tory in the afterglow of their lovemaking. "The greasepaint is making it stick up in spikes. You look like you tried to be a punker and decided against it before making a full commitment."

Full commitment, Tory thought with a frisson of alarm. Dan was using the words in a playful context, but they scared her anyway. She suspected she'd made a full commitment already. To him. Her body had, anyway. To a man she'd recognized from the beginning as her romantic waterloo.

Preferring not to let on how deeply moved and confused she'd been by the profound impact of their lovemaking, she tipped back her head and wrinkled her nose at Dan. "Thank you, Mr. Stewart. Your hair's lovely too. Not quite as dashing as the lime green wig, but quite divine in its own rumpled way."

He rolled off the bed and scooped her up in his arms in one smooth motion. "Shower time, imp."

Clasping her hands at the nape of his neck, Tory

laughed and gave her legs a perfunctory kick of protest.

Dan paid no attention. He carried her to the bathroom and put her down beside the shower stall, holding her to his side as he turned on the taps and tested the temperature. "Too hot," he said, and twisted the cold-water faucet.

Tory thrust her hand into the spray. "Now it's too cold."

"Okay, Goldilocks, you tell me when it's just right."

She grinned. When he'd made the adjustments to suit her, she nodded. "Perfect."

Dan stuck his head into the stall, then pulled back and grinned down at her, his face screwed up and his eyes squeezed almost shut against the water streaming down. "Yep. Definitely perfect."

"You're a nut," Tory said, laughing.

Dan wiped his hands over his face to get rid of the dripping water and pushed back his hair. "Okay, in you go," he ordered cheerfully with a light swat to her bottom for emphasis.

Tory obeyed, and Dan stepped in behind her.

"I've never given anyone a shampoo before," he said as he took a plastic bottle from a rack hung over the shower head.

"I could wash my own hair," Tory suggested.

Dan smiled and slowly wagged his head from side to side. "No, I'd like to do it for you. Anyway, this seems to be a day for firsts."

"What firsts?" she asked, watching him squeeze a generous dollop of shampoo into his palm.

"Shut your eyes tight," he said as he lathered her hair.

"What firsts?" Tory persisted, keeping her eyes open.

"Our first time making love, for one thing. The first time my secret identity has been discovered by someone other than Howard, for another." *And the first time I've ever experienced feelings that could shake up my whole existence,* he added silently. *The first time I've made love to a woman and wanted to keep her with me instead of making my escape as fast as decently possible. The first time I've ever believed I could have emotional staying power.*

"I wish I could hear what you're not saying," Tory remarked, intently watching him.

Dan froze and stared down at her, not quite certain she *hadn't* heard his unspoken words. But would it be so terrible if he actually told her what he felt?

Yes, he decided instantly, resuming his pleasurable task. He was treading on unfamiliar ground. He had to move carefully. It was one thing to risk getting hurt himself, but to take a chance on speaking too soon and hurting Tory later was a whole other matter. "You're a nosy little thing," he said at last, managing not to sound as strained as he felt. "You probably wish you could hear what everybody's not saying. And I told you to shut your eyes."

"Sometimes you talk in circles, you know that?" Tory commented. "But I love what you're doing, and I don't need to close my eyes. I trust you. You've very gentle."

"Too gentle?"

She giggled. "No, just right. In fact, you're so good at this I could recommend you to my hairdresser as a shampoo boy."

"There, you see?" he said with a grin. "Two job offers in one day. If my company gets swallowed up in a general reshuffling of the corporate deck, I'll have options. Shampoo boy or Tory's clown. How about you? If everything fell apart for you professionally, what would you do? Take your puppet show on the road?"

"I suppose so, but I'd really rather be . . ." She giggled, than said defiantly, "An exotic dancer."

Dan's brows shot up. "You mean a stripper?"

"I mean an exotic dancer," Tory insisted. "But the old-fashioned kind."

"Every man's dream," Dan said, rolling his eyes. "A sweet old-fashioned stripper. What would be your gimmick? Fans?" He scooped two handfuls of lather up in his palms and carefully placed them on her breasts. "Bubbles?"

"I knew you'd get the idea," Tory shot back, laughing.

"I'm getting ideas, all right," Dan said. He pulled her hard against him.

"What I like about you," Tory murmured, "is where you get your best ideas."

It took Dan a very long time to finish her shampoo.

When they finally stepped out of the shower Tory said shakily, "I don't think I'll recommend you to my hairdresser after all. You seem to have a tendency to get distracted."

Dan bundled her into a huge towel and wound a smaller one around her head. "That's okay. I'd rather be your clown."

"You'll have to be a smiling one, though. I like my clowns to smile."

"It's just as well. I think I've forgotten how to frown." Dan began drying his hair vigorously with another towel.

"That's the nicest thing you could have said to me," Tory said softly.

Dan stopped, pushed back his towel, and looked at her. She meant it, he thought with utter amazement. Another woman would want to be told how beautiful she was, how exciting a lover, how special in every way. Tory's eyes were shining because he'd said she made him forget how to frown.

Tossing aside his towel, he raked his fingers through his hair to smooth it down a little, then reached for Tory and pulled her into his arms.

All at once he was gripped by a primitive urgency, a need that went beyond the yearning for physical release. He had to make Tory his. All his. He had to make her know she belonged to him. He had to imprint himself on her very soul.

Tory, her gaze held by Dan's, sensed a change in him. His arms suddenly felt like tempered steel around her. When he lowered his head to capture her mouth, his kiss demanded her total surrender.

She was trembling with mingled shock and pleasure by the time he raised his head and looked down at her again, his eyes dark with purpose as well as passion. He reached up and unwound her makeshift turban. The simple gesture sent shivers through her, and she wasn't sure why. He took a comb from the vanity and painstakingly smoothed her hair. Tory felt treasured, yet unnerved by the complex tangle of her feelings, and though she laughed and teased him when he showed remarkable expertise with a hairdryer, the raw sensuality implicit in everything he did was overpowering.

He tugged away her towel and remained silent for endless moments, his perusal of every inch of her body a blatant act of possession. Lifting her in his arms, he carried her back to his bed and lowered her to the mattress. He stroked her hair back from her forehead and kissed her with soothing tenderness.

Then he made long, leisurely love to her, kissing and tasting, savoring and exploring, taking all her secrets and making them his. When she whispered a shy protest, he said gently, "I'm not going to hurt you, Tory. Not now, and not later. Don't hold back. There's no need. We're long past that point."

To her amazement, Tory believed him. He wouldn't hurt her. The warning he'd given her only a week before didn't matter. The seeds of doubt Howard had planted inadvertently in her mind with his chatter about Dan's history of avoiding involvement fell by the wayside. She relaxed and gave herself to him, and when Dan's tongue found the petals of her femininity, making them open like a pink hibiscus bursting into full bloom, Tory soared with the joyous liberation of her innate sensuality.

She was as soft as warmed honey when Dan covered her body with his and filled her with himself. He kissed her eyelids. He stroked his tongue over her lips and delved into her mouth. He held her and murmured tender endearments, urging her to keep letting go, keep flying higher.

As Dan's quickening movements signaled that he was edging toward his own summit, Tory suddenly felt herself being drawn into an erotic maelstrom. It frightened her. It was like finding herself in the eye of a tornado. Yet she was too exhilarated to struggle against it, and even if she'd tried to fight she knew she'd have been helpless. Clinging to Dan as she was caught up in a wild, dizzying whirl, she surrendered unequivocally. She gave up her separateness. She became part of him.

A moment later, he became part of her.

Whatever happened, Tory understood that there would be no turning back. And that thought was the one that stunned her when mindless passion inevitably gave way to returning fears. She'd taken an irrevocable step.

For once, Tory Chase hadn't left herself an escape hatch.

Dressed in shorts and a T-shirt, Dan stood at the kitchen counter tossing olive oil and red wine vinegar into a salad to go with the chicken casserole that had started to bubble in the microwave. Tory, wearing one of his shirts, was setting the table in the dining room. He watched her flitting around the mahogany table, her shirttails provocatively flying and her skin still pink from the glow of fulfillment, and he felt another spurt of sureness—at least about his own feelings.

He knew he was different with Tory than he'd ever been with any other woman. For the first time he didn't want out. He wasn't looking for a painless way to end something he wished he hadn't started.

But Tory's reaction—her innermost reaction—was a very big question mark. Dan knew she was as profoundly affected by their lovemaking as he was. He would never forget her weeping, her clinging to him, her whispering his name over and over like a litany. But eventually she'd become so quiet, so pensive.

He wished he could keep her in bed permanently. That was where he could be sure of her.

No, he corrected himself. He didn't wish any such thing. He loved Tory for everything she was, not just for her passion.

The salad utensils remained suspended in midair over the wooden bowl as Dan's own passing thought came back and hit him like a cannonball. *Did* he love Tory? How could that happen? Wasn't he the Dan Stewart who'd always believed he was incapable of love? Couldn't know the first thing about it? After all, he was a good Californian. He read his annual quota of pop-psychology books. He'd figured out that he hadn't experienced enough affection in his formative years to give him the basic skills. Love was a learned emotion, and he hadn't learned it.

Had he?

No. He hadn't learned a thing about love. It had crept up on him and hit him right between the eyes. If it hadn't caught him unawares, he'd have dodged it. He'd have reasoned it out of existence. He'd have found a way to rob it of its power because it scared the hell out of him. Always had. Always would, probably. But could he live with the unnerving reality of loving a woman? Could he live without it?

"That casserole smells so good," Tory said, returning to the kitchen.

Dan stared at her. "I'm not going to want to let you go," he heard someone say.

Tory stared back at him, her eyes huge and startled.

He realized he was the one who'd spoken. "I mean tonight," he added hastily, then frowned and tried again. "Or tomorrow night. Or . . . or any night, dammit." Resuming his salad tossing with vigorous movements that threatened to land more lettuce on the counter and floor and possibly even on the ceiling than in the bowl, he barreled ahead as if he honestly believed Tory would go along with his craziness. "I . . . I know this sounds a bit premature, but . . ." He cleared his throat. "How about staying here with me?"

"Staying with you?" Tory repeated in a small voice. "What do you mean?"

Dan stopped throwing lettuce leaves around and turned to face her. "What do I mean? I'm not sure. I guess I'm asking you to . . . to sleep in my bed, and in my arms," he said, taking both her hands in his and drawing her closer to him. "I'd like to open my eyes each morning and see you lying next to me. I want to brighten my closets by hanging your clothes beside mine . . . and brighten my days by sharing them with you."

A lump rose in Tory's throat. She did want to sleep in Dan's arms every night, to open her eyes each morning and see him lying next to her. But everything had happened so quickly. Too quickly. She wasn't ready for the kind of commitment Dan was implying. She wasn't sure what kind of commitment he *was* implying. "Stay with you for how long?" she asked after several charged moments.

Forever, Dan wanted to answer. But Tory's question and her stricken expression stopped him. "Do you think I'm rushing things a little?" he said with an embarrassed grin.

Tory was perversely disappointed by his quick retreat, but she brought herself up short. What had she expected after one torrid afternoon, especially with a man of Dan's experience? A proposal? And even if he'd offered one, she would be an idiot to take it seriously. For all she knew he was in the habit of going overboard at the beginning of a relationship and regretting his hasty words later, when he cooled down. She had to give him a chance to think things over. She needed to do some hard thinking herself.

She managed a smile. "Yes, I'd say you're rushing things a little," she said softly. "We don't know each other, Dan."

Dan didn't agree. He knew everything about Tory that counted. He believed Tory knew everything about him that really counted. But he had to admit there were a few details missing, so he understood her hesitation. He was asking her to give herself into his keeping, yet he hadn't made her feel safe. Just because his own conversion to loving instead of leaving was so sudden and so complete, he was expecting Tory to keep pace. From what he'd heard, love didn't work that way. And maybe part of learning to love was trying to open up to Tory a little—outside the bedroom. He only hoped he wouldn't do something to lose her before he won her. "Be patient with me," he said with a smile. "I'm new at this kind of thing."

"So am I," Tory admitted.

Dan kissed her hands before releasing them, then picked up the salad bowl and gave it to her to take to the dining room. "You haven't had any serious relationships?"

"Semi-serious. Not life threatening, though."

Reaching for a pair of pot holders, Dan froze. "Life threatening?"

"Life*style* threatening," Tory said with a sheepish laugh. "I guess that's what I meant."

Dan finished getting the pot holders. "I think you meant exactly what you said. All those years of being shunted from pillar to post by your father's career left their mark. Nobody's going to be in a position to run your life but you, right?"

Tory wasn't sure about even that resolve anymore, but she wasn't going to admit her confusion to Dan. Not yet. Not until she had a chance to get used to being a slightly different person from the one she'd been just a few hours earlier. So she shrugged, put on her best Mona Lisa smile, and made no comment.

"I agree," Dan said after a moment, as if she'd answered him. "Let's not get into such a heavy topic right now. It's bad for the digestion."

Tory laughed again and turned to take the salad to the dining room while Dan whisked the casserole from the microwave. Good lord, she thought. Had she really used the term *life threatening*? Was she that negative about a serious involvement?

More than negative, she had to admit. Terrified. And with good reason. She yearned to accept Dan's invitation to "stay" with him for as long as he wanted her—and she had no guarantee about the life expectancy of his desire—yet what she'd said was true. She hardly knew him. For that matter, she hardly knew herself anymore. Where was the Tory Chase who'd been so convinced she would always be in charge of her own destiny? Dear heaven, if Dan asked her to move to the South Pole to be with him, she might just dash out to buy a snowsuit and a Dale Carnegie book about how to make friends and influence penguins. But sane, mature people didn't do that sort of thing on impulse. And wasn't she a sane, mature person?

Dan was right about one thing, she decided. This topic was bad for the digestion. She hadn't even eaten yet, and her stomach was doing a manic tumbling act.

Despite her queasiness Tory sampled Dan's casserole. He seemed so proud of the dish she had to do it justice.

With the first bite, she was pleasantly surprised. Not bad, she thought, then tried a second taste, and a third. "Fabulous," she said when she'd polished off every morsel of her dinner. "Along with all your other talents, Mr. Stewart, you can count being a great cook. I'm impressed."

"I'd like to take the credit, but I can't—except for the salad, that is," Dan confessed. "My freezer's full of casseroles and baked goods and home-cooked TV dinners I didn't make. Once I learned how to operate the microwave I had this meal preparation thing aced."

"You had to learn how to operate a microwave?" Tory said, pretending to be horrified. "Daniel J. Stewart, wizard of the electronics industry, had to learn how to push the start button on a kitchen appliance?"

"Listen, I don't care who you are or what kind of company you run. Those instruction booklets are hell to follow."

After laughing and shaking her head in mock despair, Tory asked, "So who did make the casserole?" The minute the words were out she wished she could call them back. Who, indeed? A lot of women still believed in the old-fashioned route to a man's heart.

She tried to think of a way to change the subject so Dan wouldn't have to answer her stupid question, but he replied before she could come up with anything. "This dish and all the rest of the freezer goodies were part of my latest care package from Mrs. Stewart's Cozy Casseroles," he said cheerfully.

Tory's fork slipped from her fingers and clattered to her plate. "Oh," she said, staring down at it. Mrs. Stewart? Nobody had told her about a Mrs. Stewart. Dan wasn't married. She'd have known if he were married. Of course, he did live in a cozy house with antique furnishings and beautiful paintings, the colors and accents all muted pastels and earth tones that suggested a woman's touch. Even his dinnerware was bright and pretty, not at all the kind of china a man would choose on his own. A woman had been involved in putting the place together, and not just a slick decorator. Perhaps Dan had been married but was divorced. Or separated, at least. But . . .

"Tory, you're doing it again," Dan said, breaking into the turmoil of her thoughts.

She jerked her head up and faced him. "Doing what?"

"You're judging me. You're leaping to the worst possible conclusion on a thin shred of evidence.

I'm sorry about that thoughtless remark of mine, but I—"

"You mean this Mrs. Stewart is no relation?" she said with a rush of hope.

"No, that's not what I mean."

"She's your ex-wife, and you've had one of those civilized divorces?"

Dan frowned and gave her a baffled look. "What gave you an idea like that?"

"All those casseroles," Tory answered, beginning to feel foolish. Good grief, she'd have heard if Dan had ever been married. What *did* make her so eager to jump to damning conclusions about him?

Dan shook his head and heaved a deep sigh. "Look, I know I shouldn't have referred to a Mrs. Stewart without explaining who she is, but I never dreamed you'd invent a wife for me, or even an ex-wife. You know better, Tory."

She managed a feeble smile. "I guess I do. But if you've never been married, who's Mrs. Stewart? She can't be your mother."

"Why not?"

"Because you don't have a mother."

"Everybody has a mother," Dan pointed out reasonably.

"Well, of course everybody has a mother, but didn't yours deposit you on a church doorstep when you were three?"

"She was still my mother. We lost touch for a few years, that's all."

Tory searched his eyes, wondering if he was putting her on. "You mean you're . . . you're close to her? So close she makes meals to fill up your freezer?"

"She says it's her chance to catch up on all the years of cooking for me that she missed out on," Dan said, smiling.

Tory looked down at her plate. "And did she help decorate your house?"

"Right down to the salt and pepper shakers," Dan answered, his smile widening as he realized just how much had been going on in Tory's mind while he'd been sitting there being thickheaded. All her stewing meant she was jealous. And if she was jealous, he didn't have much to worry about. Eventually she would accept the inevitable.

"I had no idea," Tory said shortly after several moments of mute shock. "I simply had no idea at all that your mother was still in the picture. It never even occurred to me."

"I know, and that's my fault," Dan said. "I've felt guilty ever since our outing in Ventura. I was so busy being flip, I didn't stop to think until much later that I'd left you with the wrong impression of my mother and of the circumstances."

"What *are* the circumstances? Did your mother eventually go back and find you? Did she take you out of whatever foster home you were in?" Tory asked, her imagination instantly conjuring up a poignant moment for the little boy Dan had been.

"Actually, I went out and found her," he said. "And I was on my own by that time. All the foster homes were behind me."

"So you searched for your mother after you'd grown up?"

Dan smiled. "The truth is, I didn't start to grow up until after our reunion—or rather, our confrontation. But technically I was an adult. Eighteen. Not the age of reason for most people, and certainly not for me. I was seething with anger, and the woman who'd discarded me—which was the way I saw things then—seemed like the logical target to lash out at."

Tory felt a wrench to her insides, as if she were experiencing the pain of that eighteen-year-old.

"I'm so sorry, Dan. Sorry for all the things you've gone through, and sorry for . . ." Pausing, she gave a small laugh. "For apparently not having grown up yet myself, even though I was raised by two loving parents and have no excuse for being such a dope."

"Sure you have," Dan said, getting up to go around to her side of the table. Taking her hand, he drew her up into his arms. "You're a woman who grew up thinking it was normal to talk to hand-puppet animals."

Beginning to recognize Dan's affectionate teasing, Tory didn't even pretend to take offense. She slid her arms around his waist and rested her head on his chest. "Did you lash out at your mother when you got the chance?" she asked.

"I didn't get that chance. For some reason I let her tell me her side of the story first, and then it was game over for my anger."

"Why doesn't that surprise me?" Tory murmured.

Dan cradled her face in his palms and smiled down at her. "Doesn't it?"

"No," she said huskily, her eyes glazing over with moisture. "It doesn't surprise me one bit. You're too compassionate and caring to stay angry if there's the slightest reason not to. This time I know for certain what the *J* in your name stands for."

"It's *Jughead*, remember?"

"No. It stands for *Just Wonderful.* Daniel Just Wonderful Stewart."

He shook his head, chuckling. "I like that, but the truth is that the *J* doesn't stand for anything."

"What do you mean, it doesn't stand for anything?"

"I mean I added the initial when I went into

business. I thought it sounded more solid citizen than plain Dan Stewart."

"I guess if Harry S Truman could do it, you could," Tory reasoned. "But Harry didn't put a period after the *S*. You're tricky. You put one after the *J*."

"I didn't, to start with. Other people did, so I quit trying to correct them."

"You really don't have a middle name?"

Dan grinned. "My mother was too poor. She couldn't afford extras of anything."

A sob caught in Tory's throat without warning and tears spilled from her eyes.

"Now, there you go," Dan said, wincing. "This is why I didn't tell you last week my reason for going to San Francisco. I knew you'd get all weepy on me if I did. You're so emotional, Tory. Everything you think and everything you feel is right there in those big eyes of yours for the whole world to see."

"I suppose I could try to be less transparent," she offered, suddenly eager to do anything she could to please him.

"Don't you dare," he said. "I like you exactly the way you are, even though your tears kill me and I'll do just about anything to avoid getting them started. But I'm aware that among the rare faults of Daniel Just Wonderful Stewart is a tendency to keep his feelings too well hidden. I plan to change those ways. I'm counting on you to give me lessons."

Tory giggled. "Well, you'll learn by example if you spend much time with me."

Dan's arms tightened around her. "I plan to spend a lot of time with you, Tory. If you won't have me, I'll stand under your window and serenade you like a troubadour. . . ."

Dan gave her a quick hug and then draped one arm around her shoulders to lead her to the kitchen. "Let's get some coffee and I'll tell you all about my mother—including the business she's made a fabulous success of at a time in life when most people are looking forward to retirement."

"Mrs. Stewart's Cozy Casseroles?" Tory said.

Dan took two mugs from the cupboard and started pouring the coffee he'd put on to brew before dinner. "That's what she calls her company. We like to think of her products as comfort food for nostalgic yuppies. I get my meals on the house, of course. One of the reasons I was almost late for the children's picnic yesterday was that I had to put away all the dishes I brought home from San Francisco."

"Your mother sounds delightful," Tory said, then raised her brows as something Dan had said finally registered. "San Francisco? So you went there to see her? That's what you didn't want to tell me?"

Dan handed Tory her coffee and led the way to the living room. "Mom had to go to the hospital for a battery of tests that scared her, and I felt she shouldn't be alone. But everything came out fine, so I was able to get back here in time to play Deejay."

"Good lord," Tory murmured.

"What is it?" Dan asked, darting her an anxious look.

She curled up on the couch and pretended to study the painted-desert colors of its tasteful abstract design. "It's really nothing," she said with a fleeting smile. "Except that you're turning into a saint before my very eyes. I think I was more comfortable with you when I thought you were a . . . a rogue."

"A rogue?" Dan repeated, settling into the dusty rose leather armchair across from her and putting his feet up on the hassock. "I don't believe I've been a rogue for quite a few years, Tory, but I promise you I'm no saint. I could provide testimonials to that effect if it would help."

"That won't be necessary," she said hastily. "But maybe you could throw in a few hair-raising tales of your wasted youth when you give me your life story—which I hope you're about to do right now."

"Honey, I'll curl your hair if I do a tell all," he said with a chuckle.

"Good. Start talking."

To her surprise, he did. He took her on an emotional roller coaster ride.

Despite his matter-of-fact, quip-brightened narrative, she heard the stifled sobs of a little boy who couldn't understand where his mother had gone and why she'd left him.

She lived through the nightmares of the child who'd been taken from the foster family where he'd begun to feel safe and had been sent to another home where discipline was meted out with a stick, then on to the next family after the authorities had spotted one too many bruises.

She found her jaw clenching as a tentatively secure ten-year-old had been given up too soon by kind, affectionate foster parents because of the father's sudden illness. She saw a shell forming around the boy, and wanted to hug the young Howard for being Dan's friend.

Tory was almost cheering by the time the fifteen-year-old realized he was big enough to fight back, and she found herself worried yet strangely rooting for him when he "borrowed" cars for joyrides and joined a cult-like paramilitary gang that didn't do much besides battle with other street gangs.

Then came the day Tory had been waiting to hear about, when Dan had confronted his mother to demand why she'd walked away from him and consigned him to such a loveless existence.

"As soon as she started talking I realized she'd had no other option," he told Tory in his usual offhand way. "Mom had been a waitress, romanced by a fast-talking character on his way through town with a great line, a lot of empty promises, and a phony name. It's an old story. Stewart's her maiden name, by the way. Connie Stewart. She added the *Mrs.* for the sake of appearances. Having a baby on her own, trying to raise it decently and provide for it—hell, she just ran out of steam. Physically, I mean, as well as in every other way. She collapsed. Ended up in a charity ward in a hospital after leaving me with that minister, the one person she trusted. And he did his best. He was a good man."

"But how awful for her," Tory whispered. "For both of you."

Dan left his chair and went to sit next to Tory, pulling her into his arms. He was telling her details he'd never shared with any woman—and a few he hadn't told even to Howard. It felt good to talk to her. It felt right. "My mother always intended to find me when she got back on her feet," he went on, cradling Tory's head on his shoulder. "It never happened. The years kept slipping away, and she couldn't seem to reach the point where she felt she could give me a proper home—the kind she thought I had with foster parents. So she stayed out of my life, moving from town to town in search of some kind of break, believing I was better off without her."

Tory looked up at him. "Oh Dan . . ."

"Don't you dare," he chided, then dipped his head to kiss the damp corners of her eyes. "I've had a happy ending, remember? I pulled my life together and I have my mother back. It turns out she's one terrific lady."

"And you helped set her up in business in San Francisco," Tory suggested.

He shrugged. "Maybe I gave her a little assistance after I started being fairly successful, and I encouraged her to settle down in 'Frisco. She'd always wanted to live there. It was the least I could do to make up for the tough life she'd had."

"A saint," Tory muttered, shaking her head as if to clear it. "I've gone and fallen for a man who walks around wearing a shiny halo and could sprout wings any day now."

Dan stopped breathing. "What did you say?"

"I said I've . . ." She clamped her lips shut. Good lord, she thought. She'd blurted out her deepest feelings without realizing she was doing it. But she couldn't say it again. She had to stop and think this whole thing over.

Dan knew exactly what she'd said. He didn't care that she wasn't ready to repeat it. "Stay with me," he said with sudden urgency, turning her to face him. "Just for tonight, Tory. One night. You can handle that much commitment, can't you?"

Tory gazed up at him, wanting to stay but afraid she should go. She was only half kidding about his being a saint. Everything she'd learned about Dan made her realize that he was a man who went all out, whatever he did. There were no limits. He offered a bottomless well of affection, passion, loyalty, and forgiveness.

She, on the other hand, suddenly felt like a spoiled brat who could never measure up to his standard of loving. Handed everything all her life—everything that really mattered, she knew now—she'd felt sorry for herself for the superficial details that weren't entirely to her liking. She'd planned to arrange her existence so that loving a man wouldn't complicate anything too much. She'd thought in terms of doling out parts of herself when it was convenient.

Now she knew how things had to work if they were to work at all.

Was she up to it?

She shivered and closed her eyes against the penetrating heat of Dan's gaze.

Should she stay with him . . . for just one night?

Thirteen

Tory stayed with Dan for just one night—six nights in a row.

Each morning as she left his house to go back to her own place to change her clothes and get ready for work, he suggested something they could do together that evening, and each time she found the idea irresistible, even if it was watching a video and making microwave popcorn. They inevitably ended up making love, Dan inevitably asked her to spend "just tonight" in his bed, and she inevitably said yes.

She'd taken to carrying her toothbrush and a few other essentials in her purse, but she didn't leave them at Dan's house.

On Friday morning she looked at the date on the calendar and realized she had to say no to his plans for that evening. "I promised to help Liz with a corporate weekend function at a ranch just outside town," she said with genuine regret.

"Somebody has hired an event planner for a retreat?" Dan said, disappointed even though he'd known this kind of thing had to happen, given the nature of Tory's business.

"It's not just a brainstorming session for a few executives," Tory explained. "This one's a real production number for the top brass, their biggest clients, and everybody's spouse. Rhinestone cowboys everywhere, a mini-rodeo, a mock shootout, a monster barbecue, a barn dance—you name it, we've got it." She glanced at her watch and saw that she was running late.

"Sounds like fun," Dan commented.

Tory gulped down the last of her coffee and smiled, surprised by the hint of wistfulness in Dan's tone. Perhaps there was a Wyatt Earp hidden in the depths of every American male's psyche. "It would be fun if you were going to be there," she said, picking up her dishes as she rose from the table and headed for the kitchen. "As it is, I have a feeling Liz and I are going to wish she'd thought of a more sedate theme for this bash. The schedule is going to be insane."

"You work too hard," Dan said, frowning. When Tory merely smiled and started loading the dishwasher, Dan opened his mouth to ask if she really had to stay at the ranch until the bitter end of the event. Catching himself just in time to keep from saying a word, he pressed his lips together. He wasn't pleased by the thought of Tory sequestered with a bunch of high-powered businessmen, even if there were wives on the scene, but he knew better than to play the heavy. He had no right. And it would be the dumbest move possible with a woman who had a phobia about having to answer to someone.

Besides, Dan still remembered vividly the lesson he'd learned at a tender age when he'd caught a lightning bug and tried to keep it in a jar. Its light had gone out. By wanting to possess the creature, he'd destroyed it.

He loved Tory's light. He didn't want to do anything to dim its glow.

But he wished to hell he could pin her down and be absolutely sure she knew she belonged to him and only to him. It wasn't in his nature to go around wearing a T-shirt engraved with If-you-love-something-set-it-free platitudes. What he really wanted was for Tory to accept having someone to answer to—namely, one Dan Stewart!

They finished clearing up the kitchen, and Tory grabbed her purse in a dash for the front door. "I'd better hurry. I have two meetings this morning before I join Liz to head for the ranch." She hesitated, then said, "Would you like me to call you as soon as I get back on Sunday? I'm not sure what time, but it should be around the middle of the afternoon."

Dan was astonished that she had to ask. Would he *like* her to call? How about his urge to *demand* it? Cool it, he told himself. "That'd be nice," he said with a careful smile.

Tory opened the door and started out, then turned and rose on her toes to give Dan a peck on the cheek. "Hey, you know what? I'll miss you," she said softly.

Dan hauled her into his arms and gave her a proper kiss. A branding kiss. When he raised his head after several long, searing moments, he said lightly, "Don't you go letting any of those rustlers and hustlers lure you off to another corral, understand?"

Tory was taken aback by the fervor of his kiss and the underlying edge in his tone, but she laughed and gave him a quick hug. "You're cute, you know that?"

With a pained smile, Dan let her go. Cute. So

now he was cute as well as the sweet, dear, kind, and compassionate Saint Just Wonderful.

Tory was right. She didn't know him at all.

She waved as she climbed into her car, blissfully unaware that he secretly wanted to hog-tie her to the saddle of his life, ride off with her into the sunset, and never let her out of his sight.

It was almost five when Dan's phone finally rang on Sunday afternoon. He stopped his frantic pacing and pounced on the inanimate deliverer of good or bad news, braced to hear that there'd been an accident. Or that Tory had eloped with the winner of the mini-rodeo. Or that she'd been kidnapped by slave traders from an unknown planet.

Okay, so he had some minor insecurities to work on, he admitted to himself as he lifted the receiver to his ear. Yes, he kept expecting Tory to be taken from him just because he cared so damn much for her, a nagging dread that he recognized as a scar from his past but couldn't seem to rationalize away.

Falling in love had turned him into a crazy man. Maybe it did the same thing to everybody. And there was no question about it: He'd fallen in love. Or maybe he'd been in love with Tory long before she'd finally shown up to settle sweetly into his life. "Hel-lo," he said with ridiculous cheerfulness.

"Hi," Tory's husky voice returned. "I just walked into my apartment. Sorry I'm so late."

Dan closed his eyes and let the relief wash through him, then quickly pulled himself together. She was all right. And she was cheerful. She didn't sound like someone about to launch into a "Dear Dan" farewell. "Late!" he said with feigned nonchalance. "What time is it?"

"Nearly five," Tory answered.

Precisely four minutes and thirteen seconds to five, Dan thought, but said casually, "Really?" I had no idea. I was just puttering around here, catching up on my housework." If you could call wearing a patch in the floor in front of the phone housework, he added under his breath.

"Wearing a pretty apron and all, I suppose," she said, laughing.

Dan smiled. He loved Tory's low chuckle. Suddenly he couldn't wait to see her. But was she too tired? Was she planning to crash at home? "How was your weekend?" he asked.

"A smash hit. And not as difficult as I'd expected. Liz always has things organized better than she thinks. The reason we're back late today is that we were waylaid by three people offering us assignments—one from the company that hosted this shindig, and the others from two of their corporate guests. Liz is on cloud nine. We both are."

"And so you should be," Dan said, glad he hadn't spoiled Tory's high by letting on how hard it had been for him to keep his wild imagination in check. "Is Liz with you now?"

"Heavens, no. She's heading straight for Howard's place to give him a play-by-play."

Great, Dan thought. He liked Liz, but he wanted to be alone with Tory. He hoped Tory wanted to be alone with him. "You know," he ventured carefully, "it just so happens that Mrs. Stewart's lasagna, bottomless goblets of fine red wine, crusty bread, and free back rubs are being given out here this evening to petite brunettes with amber eyes and healthy appetites. First come, first served."

"Then I'd better hurry, huh?" Tory shot back.

Dan's lips widened in a grin. She hadn't missed a beat. She did want to be with him. He decided to push things a little. "And Tory, when you get here, will you stay with me?" He almost stopped there but decided he'd better add the traditional, playful rider. "Just for tonight, of course."

There was a long silence before Tory said, "You've never asked ahead of time before. Usually it's when you have your arms around me and I can't think about anything but wanting to keep your arms around me."

"We've reached a new stage in our relationship," Dan said firmly. "I'm asking ahead of time so you can pack an overnight bag. That way we can stay in each other's arms a bit longer tomorrow morning. It's the same level of commitment, but this time we're adding the element of premeditation. Think you can deal with that?"

"Let me premeditate about it," Tory said, then was quiet again for all of five seconds. "I'll be there within the hour," she said with exaggerated briskness. "But if any other brunettes show up ahead of me because I took time to pack, I get to give the back rub. Actually, more like a backside rub. With the toe of my boot. Got that?"

"Got it," Dan said, expelling the breath he hadn't even realized he'd been holding.

After he'd hung up his grin broadened. Progress, he thought happily. Tory was going to hang one outfit in his closet for a few hours. And he'd kept his overdeveloped streak of possessiveness under wraps. He would cure himself of that fatal flaw before she ever found out he'd had it in the first place.

Today an overnight bag, tomorrow a new tooth-brush hanging in the guest bathroom.

The woman's fate was all but sealed.

Tory swiveled from side to side in her fuchsia chair, her feet up on her desk, her head tipped back so she could see the ocean-view poster taped to the window behind her right shoulder, her elbow resting on the arm of the chair, Cecil perched on her left hand.

"There's something wrong with me," Tory muttered.

"Now *there's* a hot news flash," Cecil shot back.

"I've found the perfect man," Tory went on, ignoring the rabbit's sarcasm. As her alter ego, it was part of his function to be sarcastic. He kept her from taking herself too seriously. Of course, it had occurred to her that an adult woman who tried to sort out the jumble in her head by filtering it through a hand puppet really *couldn't* take herself very seriously. "Dan Stewart is the most perfect man in the universe," she stated.

"Stay tuned, folks," Cecil said wearily. "Maybe we'll hear something we haven't heard before."

Tory shot him a look, then returned her gaze to the soothing poster view. "When Dan and I make love, it's sublime. But . . ." She paused and let Cecil take over.

"Too sublime?" he suggested.

"Exactly." Tory heaved a great sigh, then grinned. "It's amazing how you always know what I'm thinking." She studied Cecil for a long moment, then took him off her hand and put him down. She wanted to get her head straight without a prop. No more childish games when it came to serious matters. And the question of why she and Dan were keeping up their just-for-tonight pretense was serious. On the few occasions when she had to work too late to meet him afterward, or when he had to dash off on a business trip, she missed him dreadfully and couldn't wait to be with him again. So why didn't she suggest bumping up the commitment to two nights, or three, or maybe even a week? Why wasn't she letting go of all the doubts that were getting in the way?

The whole thing had taken her by surprise, that was the problem. She was afraid of waking up one morning, deciding it was all a mistake, and wanting her old life back.

She was even more afraid Dan would wake up one morning, decide it was all a mistake, and want *his* old life back.

After eyeing Cecil for a moment, Tory picked him up again. Old habits were hard to shake. Especially bad ones. "You know, Cec, every time I go rocketing off into outer space in Dan's arms I think I'll soar forever, but as soon as I come back to earth it's as if I've lost another little piece of myself somewhere out there," she said, still finding it easier to articulate the complexity of her emotions when she had someone—something—to articulate to. "And Dan seems so passionate in bed, yet so casual otherwise. If he really cared, wouldn't he be a bit more demanding of my time? More bugged by pressures that keep me away from him? Maybe even a trifle more . . . well, possessive?"

"Uh-oh," she heard. She looked up and saw Liz standing in the open doorway. "Tory, are you talking to that silly rabbit again?"

Tory snatched the puppet off her hand. "I was practicing a new routine," she said airily. "The old one's going stale."

"Tell that to the kids who fell over laughing at that picnic three weeks ago. What's the matter? Isn't Dan treating you right?"

"Dan's treating me beautifully," Tory said. Suddenly she frowned as a shaft of reflected light caught her eye. She looked for the source. It followed Liz into the tiny office and went with her as she settled into her chair behind the opposite desk. "Good lord, Liz, what's that on your hand?"

Liz held up her left hand and waggled her finger. "I thought you'd never ask. It's pretty, isn't it?"

Leaping to her feet, Tory went over to grab the flashing hand and take a closer look. "It's gorgeous! But what does this mean?"

"What does it usually mean?" Liz said, her tone softening.

Tory met her friend's gaze. "Oh my. You and Howard . . . Oh lord. I can't say I'm surprised. I'm just . . ." She swallowed hard. "Stunned."

"So am I," Liz admitted. "Howard's the only one who seems to be taking it all in stride."

"Have you set the date?" Tory asked, still clutching Liz's hand as if she thought she might have to save her from falling off a cliff.

Liz nodded.

"When? Christmas, maybe? Or next spring? A big June wedding?"

"Try Saturday," Liz answered.

Tory stared at her. "Sure. Fine. Saturday's good. Um . . . any particular Saturday?"

"This Saturday, Tory. Four days from now."

"But . . ." Tory shook her head in disbelief and ventured a protest even though she suspected it would be useless. When Liz made up her mind, it stayed made up. "We can't possibly put a wedding together in four days," she pointed out reasonably. "If a client asked us to do such a thing, we'd have her committed."

Liz smiled. "Will you be my maid of honor, Tory? Howard's asking Dan to be best man."

"I don't think this is even legal!" Tory exploded. "There are blood tests and . . . and licenses . . . and . . . well, whatever red tape must be involved."

"It's all taken care of," Liz said calmly. "We're flying to Vegas on Saturday morning."

"You're getting married in Las Vegas? In some

tacky chapel next door to a twenty-four-hour divorce court? Why the hurry?" A startling possibility struck Tory. "Oh lord, you're not . . ."

"No, I'm not pregnant," Liz said, laughing.

"Then why are you rushing into this thing? Elizabeth Collins, you aren't the quickie-wedding type! You're supposed to have a huge church extravaganza. A ten-foot train on your gown. Something borrowed, something blue . . ."

"Which reminds me, could I borrow your little pearl earrings?"

"Liz," Tory said, her voice strangled, "are you putting me on?"

"Not at all. You know I've always loved those earrings."

Tory rolled her eyes heavenward. "Okay, okay, be funny. But don't you care about a traditional wedding?"

"After all the traditional weddings I've planned for other blushing brides, the last thing I want is to go through that kind of circus myself," Liz answered. "Howie and I will throw a party for our families later, but for our actual marriage ceremony we want something quiet and private. And I've always considered it highly romantic to get married in Vegas. It won't be tacky, I promise."

"I shouldn't have used that word. Nothing connected with you could be tacky," Tory said. "But please, please, *please* make me understand why you have to take such a drastic step so soon. How can you be absolutely certain you want to spend the rest of your life with Howard?"

"I can't make you understand," Liz said. "I can't tell you anything that will resolve your ambivalent feelings about your future with Dan." She winked at Tory. "I can't do that for you any more than Cecil can. All I can say is that this step doesn't feel drastic to me. It feels right. Natural. A foregone conclusion. Howard and I simply want to put the official stamp on the commitment we've already made. Now will you be there for us?"

Tory took a deep breath and let it out slowly. She knew she would never want a Las Vegas wedding. She'd want to be married in church in Santa Barbara with her parents on hand, a few special friends, Dan's mother, of course. . . .

Oh lord. Now what? Dan hadn't mentioned marriage. And she hadn't admitted to herself that she was thinking along those lines. Not until this moment.

"Tory?" Liz prompted. "Have I shocked you that badly?"

Tory stared at her friend, then gave her head a little shake. "No. Not at all. And of course you can borrow my pearl earrings. In fact, you can have them. Now, what would you like me to wear?"

In a side room off the chapel that was nestled into a corner of a glitzy Las Vegas hotel's top floor, Dan plucked a minuscule thread from the lapel of Howard's tux. "You have everything? The ring?"

"No," Howard said patiently. "You have the ring."

"Oh. Right." Dan patted all his pockets until he'd found the gold band, exactly where it had been when he'd checked five minutes earlier. "Everything's in place in the honeymoon suite?"

"I imagine so. You said you'd take care of it."

Dan looked stricken for a moment, then nodded. "The champagne's on ice, there are enough fresh flowers in the suite and in the chapel for a Rose Bowl parade, there's a wedding cake and several trays of hors d'oeuvres, midnight snacks in the mini-fridge. . . . Anything else?"

"I can't think of anything," Howard said.

"Good. So there's no need to panic."

Howard's lips twitched with a suppressed smile. "I'll try to stay calm."

"Right. That's important, Howard. Liz is going to be very emotional, probably strung out. A bundle of nerves. You have to be strong and protective. Her personal Rock of Gibraltar. Getting married is a big thing for a woman."

"True. It's a pretty big thing for a man too," Howard remarked, checking his watch. "So it's probably a good idea for me to show up at the altar on time."

"Right. Showing up on time is important. So what are you waiting for? Let's go."

They started toward the doorway into the chapel, but Dan stopped short and turned, planting his hands on Howard's shoulders. "Look, I have to say this. I'm the closest thing you've got to a father or even a Dutch uncle, so it's up to me to do the honors."

Howard couldn't hold back his grin. "I know quite a bit about the birds and the bees, Dan. You'd be surprised."

"Fine. But do you know about women? I mean, *really* know about them?"

"Do you?" Howard asked.

Dan shook his head and sighed heavily. "Not a damn thing. But hear me out anyway. Rule number one: Be gentle. Considerate. Tender."

"Gentle. Considerate. Tender," Howard repeated, as if memorizing the instructions.

"Rule number two: Never take her for granted. Once Liz is your wife, don't climb into your computer and get lost in your robotic blueprints and forget she's out there needing plenty of attention."

Howard nodded. "Okay, no climbing into my computer or getting lost in my blueprints. What's rule number three?"

"How do you know there's a rule number three?"

"You always have a rule number three, Dan."

Dan frowned, mulling over that remark for a moment, then gave Howard a wry smile. "I guess I do, at that. Okay, so here it is: Make sure Liz knows you're there for her, but don't smother her. Treasure your wife but never act as if you own her, because you don't. She's agreeing to share her life with you, not make you her whole life. Maybe you won't be able to help feeling overly possessive. Maybe you'll want to keep ludicrously closer tabs on her, or try to dominate her, or . . . or whatever. Just don't act on those male urges, understand? Women don't have to put up with the caveman routine, and they won't put up with it. And—"

"Rule three seems to have a lot of subsections," Howard cut in, reaching past Dan to open the chapel door. "But I get the message." He paused, then added, "And since we both know the message was aimed as much at you as at me, give me a call when it finally hits its mark. One suggestion, though. Don't discount the value of male urges too much. Women don't seem to mind 'em." He winked as he started toward the altar. "Let me know when it's my turn to be the nervous best man."

Dan stood rooted to the spot until Howard turned, grinned, and beckoned to him with a little hitch of his head.

Dan was vaguely aware that the bride was a vision in creamy satin and lace, but he saw only the maid of honor, resplendent in pale apricot silk that emphasized the amber in her eyes and the strands of gold in her softly waved hair.

Howard's elbow nudged him in the ribs at some point, and Dan realized it was time to produce the ring. After a bit of fumbling he found it, then glanced back at Tory. Her eyes, as bright with sentimental tears as he'd known they would be, glinted as well with amusement at his awkwardness. He pretended to glower at her, which only make her wrinkle up her nose and send him an impish grin.

Dan had his satisfaction a moment later. It was a double-ring ceremony, and Tory had carried Howard's wedding band on her thumb. It didn't slide off without a fight. When it finally gave in it popped into the air, and Liz, with reflexes worthy of a major-league shortstop, reached out and caught it. The ceremony continued without missing a beat.

Tory looked at Dan, her smile sheepish.

He lived up to his saintly image, raising his eyes as if checking to see whether his halo was still on straight.

But when Howard and Liz were pronounced husband and wife, the playfulness between Dan and Tory abruptly ended. Their gazes darkened and locked, and when the justice of the peace suggested that a kiss was in order Dan would have reached for Tory if the bride and groom hadn't been in the way.

The celebration in the honeymoon suite was full of warmth and ebullience, but brief. Howard and Liz had planned only one night in Las Vegas, returning Sunday morning to Ventura to spend a few days on the *Moonstruck*. Dan and Tory were scheduled to fly back to Santa Barbara on a late Saturday afternoon flight.

"Wasn't that a lovely ceremony?" Tory said as

they left the happy newlyweds late in the afternoon. "I take back every negative thing I've ever said or even thought about Las Vegas weddings. That one wasn't tacky at all." She giggled. "The honeymoon suite, on the other hand . . ."

"I liked the gold Cupid fixtures on the double-size tub," Dan commented as he pushed the elevator call button.

Tory grinned. "And the round bed with the satin sheets."

The elevator arrived and the doors slid open. As Dan and Tory stepped onto it he said, "One of the other hotels has a suite done up like a sultan's tent. Now that's what I call exotic."

Tory stared at him. "How do you know about . . ." Her head snapped around, and she suddenly found the row of numbered buttons fascinating.

Frowning, Dan studied her for a moment before it dawned on him what she was thinking. "Dammit, Tory, cut that out!"

"Cut what out?" she asked innocently, though she knew precisely what he meant.

"I'm familiar with several of the honeymoon hideaways in this crazy town because I helped Howard check them out earlier this week to pick the one he thought Liz would like best. Not because I cavorted with showgirls in heart-shaped tubs and heated waterbeds during my summers as a dealer in the casinos."

Tory grimaced, but changed her mind and lifted her chin defiantly. "Hey, I'm perfectly justified in thinking you've had a colorful past, mister. It doesn't mean I'm jumping to judgmental conclusions about the present. I just don't want to pry, okay?"

Dan's brows shot up. "Good point," he murmured.

All at once a delicious temptation popped into Tory's mind. She turned to face Dan and curl her arms around his neck. "Heart-shaped tubs? Heated waterbeds? Sultans' tents?"

He gazed down at her, his heart suddenly beating faster. "Are you thinking what I'm thinking?"

She nodded, her lips tilting upward at the corners in a slow, sultry smile.

When they reached the ground floor, Dan went straight to a pay phone and made two calls—one to the airline to change their reservations to the next afternoon, and one to the hotel where he'd seen the mirrored suite he'd have chosen if he'd been Howard.

Fourteen

Tory made some important discoveries that night in Las Vegas.

She learned that making love with Dan didn't have to involve a profound, earth-moving, shattering experience. It could be fun. Full of laughter and silliness. Frivolous joy.

She learned that she didn't have to feel as if she were being taken over by a stronger force; she could enjoy the sharing of erotic play.

And she learned that she liked mirrors.

When Dan covered her body with his and entered her with his wonderfully powerful thrusts, she could watch the rippling muscles in his back, the tightening of his sleek flanks, the fit of his hips in the cradle of her thighs. She was fascinated by the stark contrast between her paleness and his sun-gilded skin. She was thrilled by the perfect molding of her soft curves to his unyielding planes. And she was moved by the sheer beauty of the union of male and female. It wasn't ungainly. It was graceful, it was poetic, it was poignant. It was love in motion.

• • •

Dan and Tory made it to the Las Vegas airport just in time for the boarding call for their midafternoon flight to Santa Barbara.

Howard and Liz rushed up to the gate right behind them.

Tory, standing in front of Dan, saw the other couple and blanched, then turned several shades of red.

Liz gave her a wicked grin, but Howard was his usual unflappable self. "Oh, hi," he said with mild surprise. "You changed your plans, too, did you? We were having such a great time we couldn't tear ourselves away."

As Tory broke into a coughing fit, Dan patted her on the back and managed to keep a straight face. "Where are you two sitting?" he calmly asked Howard and Liz.

"Near the back of the plane," Howard answered. "You?"

"The middle." Dan smiled absently at the flight attendant as he handed her the boarding passes, then looked over his shoulder at Howard again. "You're still planning to go out on your boat?"

"Definitely," Howard answered. He turned to Tory. "And don't you worry. I'll be back in plenty of time for the Stewart Electronics sound-and-light show next weekend, and my assistants are working on the specifications I gave them for the touches you've asked for."

Tory smiled and mumbled something about knowing she could count on him, then fell silent while the others chatted about the perfect sailing weather, the likelihood of an uneventful and undelayed hop to Santa Barbara, and a string of other trivialities all the way onto the plane.

"I'm so embarrassed," Tory whispered as soon as she and Dan had settled in.

"Why?" Dan said, grinning at her as he took her hand and entwined his fingers with hers. "I don't imagine we did anything Howard and Liz didn't do."

"But they're *married*!" Tory protested. Her eyes widened and her cheeks flamed even more brightly as she realized what she'd said.

Here it is, Dan thought. The moment of truth. Was he ready for it? Was Tory? Probably not, in both cases. Nevertheless, he heard himself suggesting lightly, "Maybe we could make retroactive arrangements, just to make you feel better."

Tory frowned. "I beg your pardon?"

Dan took a deep breath and let it out on a slow count of three, then spoke calmly and deliberately. "Say the word, Tory. Just say the word."

She stared at him, not sure what he meant. She thought there was only one thing he *could* mean, but still she wasn't sure.

The flight attendant broke the spell by appearing beside Dan, smiling warmly at him and less warmly at Tory, and proffering a tray of candies. Tory took a cellophane-covered lemon drop. Her hands shook as she unwrapped it. She popped it into her mouth and crunched down on it. "Good lord, I nearly broke a tooth," she said.

Dan smiled. It wasn't precisely the answer he'd hoped for, but he had to admit his proposal had been a trifle ambiguous.

And Tory hadn't said no.

Since the working principle of his life had been that the absence of a no could be the beginning of a yes, he sat back to enjoy the trip, his hopes flying higher than the aircraft at its top cruising altitude.

• • •

Dan strolled into the convention room of the hotel overlooking the Santa Barbara waterfront, where the main event of the Stewart Electronics product launch was in progress.

He was tense. He wanted to like everything Happenings had put together. He wanted this particular sales meeting to be the biggest success in his company's history as much because Tory had planned it as because it was crucial to the firm's future.

He spoke to each of the staff members at the guest registration desk, briefly wondering why there seemed to be several more of them than usual.

Then, just at the entrance to the rows of booths where each new item was displayed, he stopped in his tracks. On a large movable screen, Benjamin Franklin was beckoning to him.

Dan looked around, noticing that a few of the workers on the desk had walkie-talkies, as did one of Howard's junior technicians standing behind the screen. In fact, there seemed to be company personnel armed with communications devices and remote-control hand units stationed throughout the room.

"That's right, I'm talking to you," Ben Franklin said, pushing his little round glasses farther up on his nose and leaning forward as if to take a closer look at Dan. "Come in, my friend. Come and find out what we started that day my wife told me to go fly a kite. There are wonders here. You'll see good old American know-how at its best." Smiling, he waved his hand toward the exhibits with a dramatic flourish.

Dan laughed, already pleased. He moved on a bit and stood back to watch as one of his most important distributors was greeted by a Ben Franklin message—and not the same one he'd been given, Dan noticed with approval. Variety would keep the ploy from being too gimmicky.

From then on it was all razzle-dazzle, fun without being silly. This was no send-up, *Jetsons* style. This was solid information presented with a light touch.

When it came to indicating some of the future directions of Stewart Electronics by showing what the household robots at various stages of development could do, Tory had given them all name badges and worked them into the exhibit instead of simply putting them on display. They conducted guided tours and mini-seminars, served refreshments in the area of the room that had been set up for that purpose with a buffet table and bar, and rolled around the hall keeping everything tidy.

All the product lines were presented with the same kind of flair, crowd-pleasing humor, and infectious sense of excitement.

As the order books for available items started filling up at a record pace and dealers requested further information about the lines still being developed, all Dan wanted to do was find Tory to tell her how proud he was of the way she'd handled everything.

He wondered, as he'd wondered often during the past few days, why he still hadn't found the courage to smash through his maddening hesitance and properly ask Tory to marry him, instead of hinting at the possibility and hoping she'd take the initiative. He knew what was wrong with him, of course. His old dread of rejection. What if she turned him down? Why take the chance of spoiling what they already had by pushing for more?

He spotted Howard working the remote for Stan

and Ollie as they served canapés in the vicinity of the bar. Dan gave his friend the thumbs-up sign, which Howard acknowledged with a slight nod worthy of royalty.

Chuckling to himself, Dan went on searching for Tory. He finally spied her, her red dress a flashing beacon in the midst of the crowd. But every time he started toward her, she dashed off somewhere else, always on the move to make sure everything was humming along like clockwork.

When he finally did run her down and lead her off to a quiet corner, she beamed at him. "I think it's going well, Dan," she whispered, as if sharing a very private confidence.

"I think so too," he whispered back, his love for her welling up inside him, ready to spill over. "Stewart Electronics should be on solid ground for some time to come, thanks to you."

"I can't take the credit," Tory said, laughing and shaking her head. "It's easy to present terrific products. This job has been a cinch." She glanced around the room, surveying the happy results of all her planning. Suddenly her smile faded. She gasped. "Oh dear. There could be a little mishap in the making."

Dan followed her gaze and saw what was developing. The new Mrs. Beecher had just walked into the room. Howard was grinning from ear to ear as he waved to Liz with a remote-control unit, and in the next instant one of the robots was veering away from where he belonged, rolling into the throng in front of the display booths. It was Stan. Not that it made any difference, Dan thought, watching in horror as the robot, bearing a tray of exotic canapés, headed straight for a very important customer.

Dan wasn't sure whether to try to get Howard's

attention or throw himself into the path of the runaway robot.

A few people had become aware of the unusual situation, but they were watching with interested smiles, as if they thought the scene was part of the show.

Dan decided he had to act, and act fast. Maybe he could get hold of Stan and divert him before he mowed down half a dozen key clients.

But as Dan started forward in the hope of warding off disaster he heard a familiar voice ring out, "Stanley, stop that this instant!"

To Dan's amazement, the robot stopped and remained exactly where it was, like a raw recruit waiting for the drill sergeant's next order.

The onlookers drew a collective breath, then laughed and applauded enthusiastically.

Dan blinked. He turned to gape at Tory.

She grinned and lifted her shoulders in a modest shrug. "How's that for a hint of the versatility of these robots?" she said to the appreciative crowd. "We've just demonstrated how a remote control can be switched instantly to voice activation, allowing easy correction of a reconsidered command."

Everyone clapped again, then returned to touring the exhibit.

Howard, finally noticing what he'd done, laughed and blew a kiss to Tory.

Tory grinned again at Dan, wondering why he was looking at her so strangely. She launched into a hasty explanation. "Howard and I have been fooling around with voice activation. We were playing with the idea of making Stan obey commands from Ollie, so Stanley is programmed to obey *my* voice—at least, my voice imitating Oliver Hardy's. I wasn't sure it would work, actually. I just went ahead and did it and hoped for the best."

Dan kept staring at her, not saying a word. *Went ahead and did it and hoped for the best,* he repeated silently. The secret formula for living. The secret formula for loving.

"Dan? Are you a bit shaken? You needn't be. There was never a serious problem," Tory said, frowning at him as he stood there in an apparent trance. "Stanley is also designed to stop immediately if he comes into contact with anything—or anyone."

What a crazy incident to push him over the edge, Dan thought. What an odd reason to decide he would risk rejection or anything else he had to risk to make this woman his wife. What an offbeat way to learn that loving Tory was as natural to him as breathing, that he didn't have to worry and pretend so much, hold in so many of his feelings. He loved her. Genuinely, truly loved her. If she loved him—and he believed she did—everything else would work out.

"I can see it all now," he said, reaching for Tory's hands and drawing her close to him. "At our golden anniversary celebration, when people ask me whether there was a specific moment when I knew I had to ask you to marry me, I'll have to tell them it was right after you did the cutest Oliver Hardy impression I've ever heard."

Tory started to laugh, then stopped abruptly as all of Dan's words filtered through to her brain. "What did you say?" she whispered.

"I love you, Tory. I thought I didn't know how to love, didn't have the ability. But with you I haven't the ability *not* to love."

Tory didn't remember ordering fireworks for this event, but she was certain they were exploding all around her. "What a time for you to revert to your habit of talking in circles," Tory said softly. "But it's okay. I understand you. Love is a great translator—and I love you, Dan Stewart. I love all that you are, and have been, and will be."

Dan was beginning to hear choirs and bells again, and a brass band thrown in for good measure. Tory loved him. He decided he liked Frank Capra movies after all. Happy endings, sentimentalism, the whole thing. Tory loved him. "Are you sure about that last part?" he asked with a teasing smile. "All that I am, and have been, and will be might turn out to be a little different from what you think."

Her eyes lit up with mischief. "Please, no more warnings."

"You don't want to hear about how overbearing I am?"

"No problem. I already know."

"Or how possessive I am? Deejay isn't my only secret identity. I've been hiding all sorts of character flaws from you."

Her smile widened. "Promise?"

He drew her a little closer. "That's one thing I can promise for certain. I'm no saint, Tory. Far, far from it."

"I'm so glad, Dan. Saints and I don't . . . well . . ."

"Mesh?" he suggested.

Tory giggled. "Was I insufferable that first day?"

"No, *I* was insufferable. You're getting us confused with each other. Which leads me to think we mesh pretty well after all."

With her heart in her eyes, Tory held her breath and gazed at Dan, for once thrilled to see his smile fade, his expression grow serious.

"Will you marry me, Tory?" he asked quietly.

A lump formed in her throat. She couldn't speak. Tears filled her eyes and brimmed over, spilling down her cheeks.

"Shall I consider this a yes?" Dan said.

Tory sniffed and nodded. She tried to give him her answer in words, but couldn't.

Enfolding her in his arms, Dan smiled and didn't bother trying to blink back the dampness in his own eyes. "There's one other thing I can promise you, Mrs. Stewart–to–be. From this day on I'll make a lifelong study of the art of loving."

Tory finally found her voice. "You dear, sweet, beautiful, silly man, haven't you caught on yet to the truth? You're one of the great masters of that art. Ask Howard. Ask your mother. Ask all those kids who are so crazy about Deejay. And . . . ask me. You're the most loving person I've ever known." She gave a husky little laugh as she added, "If you don't believe all those sources, try the one nobody argues with. He'll tell you."

Lowering his head to touch his lips to Tory's, Dan murmured, "Which reminds me. Do you think Cecil will give us his blessing?"

Tory sighed and melted against her all-time favorite client—and her till-the-end-of-time love. "He will if I have anything to say about it."

THE EDITOR'S CORNER

Next month's lineup sizzles with BAD BOYS, heroes who are too hot to handle but too sinful to resist. In six marvelous romances, you'll be held spellbound by these men's deliciously wicked ways and daring promises of passion. Whether they're high-powered attorneys, brash jet jockeys, or modern-day pirates, BAD BOYS are masters of seduction who never settle for anything less than what they want. And the heroines learn that surrender comes all too easily when the loving is all too good. . . .

Fighter pilot Devlin MacKenzie in **MIDNIGHT STORM** by Laura Taylor, LOVESWEPT #576, is the first of our BAD BOYS. He and David Winslow, the hero of DESERT ROSE, LOVESWEPT #555, flew together on a mission that ended in a horrible crash, and now Devlin has come to Jessica Cleary's inn to recuperate. She broke their engagement years before, afraid to love a man who lives dangerously, but the rugged warrior changes her mind in a scorchingly sensual courtship. Laura turns up the heat in this riveting romance.

SHAMELESS, LOVESWEPT #577, by Glenna McReynolds, is the way Colt Haines broke Sarah Brooks's heart by leaving town without a word after the night she'd joyfully given him her innocence. Ten years later a tragedy brings him back to Rock Creek, Wyoming. He vows not to stay, but with one look at the woman she's become, he's determined to make her understand why he'd gone—and to finally make her his. Ablaze with the intensity of Glenna's writing, **SHAMELESS** is a captivating love story.

Cutter Beaumont *is* an **ISLAND ROGUE**, LOVESWEPT #578, by Charlotte Hughes, and he's also the mayor, sheriff, and owner of the Last Chance Saloon. Ellie Parks isn't interested though. She's come to the South Carolina island looking for a peaceful place to silence the demons that haunt her dreams—and instead she finds a handsome rake who wants to keep her up nights. Charlotte masterfully resolves this trouble in paradise with a series of events that will make you laugh and cry.

Jake Madison is nothing but **BAD COMPANY** for Nila Shepherd in Theresa Gladden's new LOVESWEPT, #579. When his sensual gaze spots her across the casino, Jake knows he must possess the temptress in the come-and-get-me dress. Nila has always wanted to walk on the wild side, but the fierce desire Jake awakens in her has her running for cover. Still, there's no hiding from this man who makes it his mission to fulfill her fantasies. Theresa just keeps coming up with terrific romances, and aren't we lucky?

Our next LOVESWEPT, #580 by Olivia Rupprecht, has one of the best titles ever—**HURTS SO GOOD**. And legendary musician Neil Grey certainly knows about hurting; that's why he dropped out of the rat race and now plays only in his New Orleans bar. Journalist Andrea Post would try just about anything to uncover his mystery, to write the story no one ever had, but the moment he calls her *"chère,"* he steals her heart. Another memorable winner from Olivia!

Suzanne Forster's stunning contribution to the BAD BOYS month is **NIGHT OF THE PANTHER**, LOVESWEPT #581. Johnny Starhawk is a celebrated lawyer whose killer instincts and Irish-Apache heritage have made him a star, but he's never forgotten the woman who'd betrayed him. And now, when Honor Bartholomew is forced to seek his help, will he give in to his need for revenge . . . or his love for the only woman he's ever wanted? This romance of smoldering anger and dangerous desire is a tour de force from Suzanne.

On sale this month from FANFARE are four terrific novels. **DIVINE EVIL** is the most chilling romantic suspense novel yet from best-selling author Nora Roberts. When successful sculptor Clare Kimball returns to her hometown, she discovers that there's a high price to pay for digging up the secrets of the past. But she finds an ally in the local sheriff, and together they confront an evil all the more terrifying because those who practice it believe it is divine.

HAVING IT ALL by critically acclaimed author Maeve Haran is a tender, funny, and revealing novel about a woman who does have it all—a glittering career, an exciting husband, and two adorable children. But she tires of pretending she's superwoman, and her search for a different kind of happiness and success shocks the family and friends she loves.

With **HIGHLAND FLAME**, Stephanie Bartlett brings back the beloved heroine of HIGHLAND REBEL. In this new novel, Catriona Galbraid and her husband, Ian, depart Scotland's Isle of Skye after they're victorious in their fight for justice for the crofters. But when a tragedy leaves Cat a widow, she's thrust into a new struggle—and into the arms of a new love.

Talented Virginia Lynn creates an entertaining variation on the taming-of-the-shrew theme with **LYON'S PRIZE**. In medieval England the Saxon beauty Brenna of Marwald is forced to marry Rye de Lyon, the Norman knight known as the Black Lion. She vows that he will never have her love, but he captures her heart with passion.

Sharon and Tom Curtis are among the most talented authors of romantic fiction, and you wouldn't want to miss this chance to pick up a copy of their novel **THE GOLDEN TOUCH**, which LaVyrle Spencer has praised as being "pure pleasure!" This beautifully written romance has two worlds colliding when an internationally famous pop idol moves into the life of a small-town teacher.

The Delaneys are coming! Once again Kay Hooper, Iris Johansen, and Fayrene Preston have collaborated to bring you a sparkling addition to this remarkable family's saga. Look for **THE DELANEY CHRISTMAS CAROL**— available soon from FANFARE.

Happy reading!

With best wishes,

Nita Taublib

Nita Taublib
Associate Publisher
LOVESWEPT and FANFARE

OFFICIAL RULES TO WINNERS CLASSIC SWEEPSTAKES

No Purchase necessary. To enter the sweepstakes follow instructions found elsewhere in this offer. You can also enter the sweepstakes by hand printing your name, address, city, state and zip code on a 3" x 5" piece of paper and mailing it to: Winners Classic Sweepstakes, P.O. Box 785, Gibbstown, NJ 08027. Mail each entry separately. Sweepstakes begins 12/1/91. Entries must be received by 6/1/93. Some presentations of this sweepstakes may feature a deadline for the Early Bird prize. If the offer you receive does, then to be eligible for the Early Bird prize your entry must be received according to the Early Bird date specified. Not responsible for lost, late, damaged, misdirected, illegible or postage due mail. Mechanically reproduced entries are not eligible. All entries become property of the sponsor and will not be returned.

Prize Selection/Validations: Winners will be selected in random drawings on or about 7/30/93, by VENTURA ASSOCIATES, INC., an independent judging organization whose decisions are final. Odds of winning are determined by total number of entries received. Circulation of this sweepstakes is estimated not to exceed 200 million. Entrants need not be present to win. All prizes are guaranteed to be awarded and delivered to winners. Winners will be notified by mail and may be required to complete an affidavit of eligibility and release of liability which must be returned within 14 days of date of notification or alternate winners will be selected. Any guest of a trip winner will also be required to execute a release of liability. Any prize notification letter or any prize returned to a participating sponsor, Bantam Doubleday Dell Publishing Group, Inc., its participating divisions or subsidiaries, or VENTURA ASSOCIATES, INC. as undeliverable will be awarded to an alternate winner. Prizes are not transferable. No multiple prize winners except as may be necessary due to unavailability, in which case a prize of equal or greater value will be awarded. Prizes will be awarded approximately 90 days after the drawing. All taxes, automobile license and registration fees, if applicable, are the sole responsibility of the winners. Entry constitutes permission (except where prohibited) to use winners' names and likenesses for publicity purposes without further or other compensation.

Participation: This sweepstakes is open to residents of the United States and Canada, except for the province of Quebec. This sweepstakes is sponsored by Bantam Doubleday Dell Publishing Group, Inc. (BDD), 666 Fifth Avenue, New York, NY 10103. Versions of this sweepstakes with different graphics will be offered in conjunction with various solicitations or promotions by different subsidiaries and divisions of BDD. Employees and their families of BDD, its division, subsidiaries, advertising agencies, and VENTURA ASSOCIATES, INC., are not eligible.

Canadian residents, in order to win, must first correctly answer a time limited arithmetical skill testing question. Void in Quebec and wherever prohibited or restricted by law. Subject to all federal, state, local and provincial laws and regulations.

Prizes: The following values for prizes are determined by the manufacturers' suggested retail prices or by what these items are currently known to be selling for at the time this offer was published. Approximate retail values include handling and delivery of prizes. Estimated maximum retail value of prizes: 1 Grand Prize ($27,500 if merchandise or $25,000 Cash); 1 First Prize ($3,000); 5 Second Prizes ($400 each); 35 Third Prizes ($100 each); 1,000 Fourth Prizes ($9.00 each) ; 1 Early Bird Prize ($5,000); Total approximate maximum retail value is $50,000. Winners will have the option of selecting any prize offered at level won. Automobile winner must have a valid driver's license at the time the car is awarded. Trips are subject to space and departure availability. Certain black-out dates may apply. Travel must be completed within one year from the time the prize is awarded. Minors must be accompanied by an adult. Prizes won by minors will be awarded in the name of parent or legal guardian.

For a list of Major Prize Winners (available after 7/30/93): send a self-addressed, stamped envelope entirely separate from your entry to: Winners Classic Sweepstakes Winners, P.O. Box 825, Gibbstown, NJ 08027. Requests must be received by 6/1/93. DO NOT SEND ANY OTHER CORRESPONDENCE TO THIS P.O. BOX.